Dr. Chase Hudson

-

Jessica Gadziala

Dedication:

To Heather(QueenOfBooks) who loved
Chase even more than I did and convinced me
to tell the world his whole story. She's the best.
I am grateful for all her excitement and
(somewhat constant) forceful "suggesting" (which
she has told me can no way be confused with "nagging")
that kept me on track.
She's called "dibs" on Chase by the way.
Don't try to steal her man- she'll cut you.
:)

Before the Sessions

Her file was handed to me in a sealed envelope. I moved to the waiting area, breaking the seal and pulling out the paperwork.

Ava Davis. Twenty seven.

Young. That was really young for a typical surrogate client.

She had a long history of panic attacks and generalized anxiety, selective mutism, and slight OCD. All of which she had opted to treat with talk and exposure therapy instead of medicine.

I skimmed over her medical records. There was nothing of real importance save for a broken ankle when she was twelve, so I skipped right to the sexual questionnaire in the back.

Describe, in detail, what you believe is the root of your dysfunction:

My first sexual encounter was awkward and painful. So painful that I got sick. My boyfriend at the time freaked out, started cursing, telling me I ruined it for him. And ever since then, I just... can't let someone touch me because touching leads to sex, sex leads to pain, and pain leads to men getting really angry with me when I (inevitably) disappoint them.

Christ.

Point one for the dickhead first boyfriend. Screwed her up for life while he got to go on and live a normal sex life, surely disappointing every woman whose legs spread for him.

How many sexual partners have you had:

Four.

Four. One would assume her pattern just kept repeating, adding more and more anxiety to a situation she was already uncomfortable with. All of that finally got her to the point of desperation which forced her to seek help. My kind of help.

It really said something about how determined she was to get better. Because women didn't, almost as a rule, turn to sexual surrogacy. It wasn't that women had much lower rates of sexual dysfunction than men, it was that society made it impossible for them to seek help.

Women were stripped of their innate complicated sensuality to allow them to become hollow sex symbols. Every magazine on the newsstand was shouting about hour-long orgasms, multiple orgasms, and how to please your man. They made it infinitely clear to women that their place in life was to cater to the sexual needs of male partners who generally proved

5

inadequate in delivering the promised multiple or hour-long orgasms, further devaluing the woman's self worth.

Without them even realizing it, they are being assaulted with an impossible standard daily.

And it screwed with their heads.

It made women who would normally be able to achieve an orgasm in the right situation believe she was physically incapable of them.

Or it made them believe they owned their sexuality and could have multiple sexual partners and no one would think the lesser of them whilst simultaneously slut-shaming them in a society that still, underneath all the "sex sells" mentality, held virginity as the ideal.

The number of women truly dealing with sexual dysfunction was at least three times what the statistics suggested. They were just too embarrassed or too uninformed of the possibility of getting better to seek out professional help.

My surrogacy practice was a testament to that fact.

I had been doing it alongside my normal psychology practice for about a decade. I had a total of twelve clients. I averaged about one per year.

Twelve women. In a city where hundreds were suffering.

My clients were generally referred to me by other psychologists who had patients they realized were dealing with dysfunction. I was the only game in town. Hell, I was the only male surrogate in three states.

Ava Davis was referred by Dr. Bowler, someone she had been seeing for years. She had tried more traditional approaches with Ava, with efforts to bolster her confidence, make her more sexually literate. Nothing had worked.

I closed her file and slipped it back into the envelope. I move behind the reception desk, pressing a few buttons, increasing the heat in the next room and play some soft music. Then I made my way to my office door and went in.

DR CHASE HUDSON

Introductory Session

I was prepared for her anxiety. I had been ready for her to be sitting ramrod straight, for her hands to be spread out on the cushions beside her, and for her head to snap up in my direction like a scared deer when the door closed.

All of that, I had expected.

What I hadn't expected was for her to be the prettiest fucking thing to ever set foot in my office.

She was slightly taller than average with long legs and an average body type. Not skinny. Not especially curvy either. Her face, though...

It was soft and feminine, dominated by big brown eyes and framed by long blonde hair, a little beach-wavy. She had a lower lip that plumped slightly out, just begging to be kissed.

Her eyes were on me, taking me in, her features a mix of relief and utter discomfort.

"Miss Davis," I said, my voice coming out a little tighter than normal.

"Dr. Hudson," she greeted in an even more tense tone, pushing her hands off the cushions and moving to stand.

"Chase," I said automatically, shaking my head. "Don't get up," I said, holding up a hand and moving across the room to the alcove where she was seated. I put her paperwork down on the side table and sat in the chair across from her, my head tilting, watching her. Her anxiety was already spiking. Her breathing was coming out shallowly, her lips slightly parted, her eyes a little wide. "Can I call you Ava?" I asked, but she wasn't paying attention. I could practically hear her mind racing. "Ava," I broke in, my voice firmer than normal.

Her eyes snapped to mine. "Sorry," she rushed immediately, shaking her head. "I just..."

"You're nervous," I said, shrugging a shoulder.

"Yeah," she admitted, her breath airy.

"We're just talking. Think of this as any normal therapy session, okay?"

"Okay," she agreed, sucking in a slow breath and letting it out just as slowly, trying to calm herself down. It didn't seem to be working.

"Your chart says you started therapy when you were fifteen for anxiety issues," I observed, trying to get her mind off the very prominent elephant in the room for a moment.

"Yes."

"And now you are..." I started, and she quickly cut me off.

"Twenty-seven."

"Any success with the treatment?" I asked, already sensing that the answer would be a resounding 'no' given how tense she was just talking to me.

She made a half-laugh, half-snort sound, running a hand through her long hair, making it fall more to one side than the other. "Yes and no. Every time I get over one thing that makes me anxious..."

"A new anxiety develops," I supplied, knowing it was the answer. It was always the answer. Afraid of crowded stores? We fix that and suddenly you can't stand to be out in an open field. Anxiety was a bitch of a disorder to treat.

"Yup," she agreed, nodding a little. Her shoulders had dropped slightly. I was sure it was subconscious, but she was losing a little bit of her tension.

"That must be incredibly frustrating."

"You have no idea," she said, an edge to her tone.

"What are your current anxieties?"

"I have issues feeling trapped," she started immediately, the words rote, like she had said them a million times. "So work can be a problem. Someone else driving me, especially public transportation. Public speaking and..."

Her words trailed off, her cheeks getting a little pink, her shoulders tensing right back up. Embarrassed. She was too embarrassed to admit she was anxious about sex.

"And sex," I supplied for her.

"Yeah," she said, her blush getting darker.

"Okay," I went on, casual, trying to put her at ease. "I read in your chart that you don't ever remember not having a phobia about sex."

"Right."

"But you have tried to get more comfortable with it," I observed, thinking of the number of sexual partners she listed.

To this, she let out a tight little laugh, sounding nervous and somehow self-deprecating at the same time. "Exposure therapy," she suggested.

Caught off guard, I laughed. It was a low rumbling sound that made her eyes shoot to mine, her brows drawing together. "With no success though," I went on.

"No."

"Yet you kept trying."

"Yeah," she said, looking down at her hands. The air around her seemed to get heavy. Almost sad.

"So why are you here?" I asked, wanting to catch her off guard.

It worked. Her head shot up, her gaze found mine, hers looking confused for a moment before settling into what could only be described as annoyed. Like she was angry at me for making her tell me.

"I'm... frigid," she answered after a long silence.

"Are you?" I asked automatically, bending forward toward her, resting my elbows on my knees. I was trying to get into her space, trying to gauge her reaction to my proximity. "Being frigid implies an absence of interest in sex and a lack of sexual fantasies," I explained.

"Oh," she breathed out, looking somewhere near a six on the discomfort scale.

"Seeing as you are here," I went on, fighting a smile at the way her eyes kept moving over my features, "I wouldn't call you frigid."

"Okay," she agreed without even thinking about it.

"Do you have sexual fantasies, Ava?" I asked and watched her eyes go almost comically wide. If she wasn't so utterly panicked and uncomfortable, it would have been cute.

Her eyes dropped automatically downward, resting on my arm somewhere. There was something else though. Her thighs pressed more firmly together. It was a telltale sign of arousal. She wanted me.

Fuck.

That was good. From a professional standpoint, that was a good thing. It would make the process easier for both of us.

But from a personal standpoint... it made it complicated. Because I fucking wanted her too. It was not in a professional "I need to get it up so I can help them get better" kind of way. It was in a very cut and dried 'If I saw her in a bar, I'd have been buried deep in her pussy five minutes from meeting her' kind of way.

"Yes," she finally admitted, snapping me out of my image of her beneath me just before it got really obvious where my mind was.

"Do you get turned on?" I asked, already knowing my answer.

"Yes," she said again, her voice barely a whisper.

"Good," I said, watching the top of her head. "Ava, can you look at me?" It took her a few seconds, but she forced her head up. "There you are," I said, giving her a small smile. "It's good that you get turned on," I explained. "This process will be much easier because you do. Now, I'm sure you did some looking around on my website, but would you like a bit more in-depth information on how this works?"

"Sure," she said in a tone that suggested she'd rather get exfoliated by a cheese grater than have me keep talking.

"Today we talk," I explained, though talking was the last thing I wanted to be doing. "If all goes well and you are comfortable enough with the situation, we will set up the date for your next session. Each session will gradually increase in intimacy. Provided things go par for the course, sex will likely happen around the sixth session."

She looked a mix of relieved and anxious. "Okay. Wh... what will the first five sessions be then?"

She stammered.

Actually stammered.

And, damn if it wasn't one of the cutest things I had ever heard.

I offered her a small smile. "The first session is just getting comfortable with contact. At most, it will be kissing. From there, the next session will include undressing. You will learn to get comfortable with your nudity as well as... someone else's."

I almost said 'mine' and carefully skirted around it at the last second. From the look of panic on her face, I might as well have not even bothered. She was already thinking about it. Normally, it would be pretty hot to realize she was thinking about me and her naked together. But when she looked as stricken as she did right then, yeah, there was nothing sexy about that.

"Ava, don't go there." I reached out, putting my hand down on her knee, trying to ground her, bring her back to the present. "Anxiety doesn't exist in the moment. It is only in the past and the future. So, let's not think about those things, alright? Just be in the moment." Her gaze went pointedly to my knee. "This moment makes you uncomfortable, doesn't it?" I asked, squeezing her knee slightly.

Her eyes rose from my hand on her knee to look me in the eye. "Yes."

"But not enough to push me away," I observed.

"Not yet," she admitted and I felt myself chuckle, letting my hand drop.

"The purpose of this is to push you out of your comfort zone. It's important that you don't push me away with the first twinge of anxiety. As I'm sure you learned in your previous therapy sessions, anxiety can really only be treated with exposure to that which makes you anxious."

"Right."

"So if kissing makes you anxious..." I prompted.

"I have to let you kiss me."

I hadn't expected her to say it. I had expected her to hedge. Or to shut down. To slip momentarily into the mutism. At her words, I felt my eyes slip to her lips for the barest of seconds, thinking of them underneath mine, feeling the desire well up strong and insistent.

I took a breath, pushing those feelings away.

"Exactly," I said, sitting back. I needed the space. I needed to put the professional line back into place. "Only pull away or push me away if you can't talk yourself down. When you get to the point where you can't take it anymore. That being said, I am going to be communicating with you the entire time, trying to work to dispel the fears before they become overwhelming. The point is for you to get to the point where you can enjoy being touched."

As soon as the words were out of my mouth, I could see the range of emotions overcoming her face. Most prominently, there was panic. She was freaking out about being touched. Specifically, about me touching her. That was to be expected, but it didn't make it any less troubling.

"You're a very beautiful woman," I heard myself say, inwardly cringing at the words. It was unprofessional to talk her up. To, essentially, hit on her. But at the same time, she was obviously struggling with her self-esteem and I wanted to get a clear image of how much she was suffering.

"I'm sorry?" she asked, brows drawing together, making two small vertical lines fold above her nose. Like she was confused. Like she thought she misheard me.

"I said you are a very beautiful woman," I repeated, watching as something very different from confusion take over her features. If I wasn't mistaken, it was frustration, bordering on anger.

"Compliments make you uncomfortable?" I asked, already knowing the answer, but needing her to say it.

"Yes."

"Why?" I asked, watching her squirm in her seat, knowing she was getting close to shutting down on me. "Because you don't believe them?" I offered her the olive branch.

"Yes," she said, looking relieved to not have to spell it out.

"Ava," I said, my voice a little firm. "I don't feed women compliments for fun. If I tell you something, I mean it. It is an observation. You are a beautiful woman. Case closed." It was a fact. She was beautiful. There was no question about it. Her being unaware of it just made her all the more attractive.

"Right," she said in an odd tone. Disbelieving, maybe a little annoyed.

I couldn't help it. My lips twitched then shifted up to a smirk. She really had no idea. Her steadfast determination to not accept a simple fact was at once frustrating and adorable. "Ava, what do you think the main reason men compliment women is?" I asked, letting there be a pause before going on. "To get women into bed." I leaned forward, my smile getting a little bigger. "You are here to go to bed with me. Eventually. Do you really think I need to give you compliments?"

"I guess not," she said, but I could tell she was only half believing me.

I fought a laugh. "Exactly. So, you're beautiful. It's a biological fact." As soon as I finished, I watched her grasp at straws, trying to make herself believe that I didn't actually think she was gorgeous, that I was just saying she had good genes. "And I find you incredibly attractive," I added, watching her practically pout.

"Thanks," she mumbled, her eyes moving from mine.

I felt myself chuckle. I couldn't help it. "Do you find me attractive?" I asked, expecting a pause, a mumble, a tripping of words.

She answered immediately and clearly. "I think the entire continental US would find you attractive."

Oh, yeah. She was good. That was quick. To anyone else, it would have been a satisfactory answer. But I couldn't let her get away with it.

"That's wonderful," I said, leaning closer, "but I wasn't asking the entire continental US, I was asking you."

Her eyes slid slightly to the side, making it appear that she was still giving contact, when, in fact, she was looking at my earlobe. "Yes," she admitted in a quiet voice.

She was done.

I had pushed her far enough for the intro session. If I kept going, she would shut down and then not come back.

"Good," I said, getting out of my chair and moving out of the seating alcove. "So, I will see you... Tuesday for your first session." It was a half-declaration, half-question, giving her the chance to object though I knew she wouldn't.

"Okay."

"Okay," I repeated, opening the door and stepping into the space, waiting for her to follow. She did, making sure her body didn't so much as brush mine in the process. "Seven at night work for you?"

There was the barest of pauses. "Yes."

My hand lifted, pressing into her lower back, trying to see her reaction as I led her into the waiting room. She tensed, but only slightly. I let her go as soon as I walked up to the reception desk.

"See you then, Ava."

Something flashed across her face. It was too quickly gone to decipher before she mumbled awkwardly, "Okay," as she went out the door.

After the Session

I should have recused myself.

I knew it the second I closed myself back up in my office when she left.

It was unprofessional to go on, to work with a woman I was more than professionally interested in.

Desire may have, in a way, been a part of the process. It was supposed to be in a detached sort of way, a thing I managed to have happen so I could help my clients. It wasn't meant to be the point of it all.

But there was no mistaking it, I was attracted to Ava.

As in... I wanted to know what she sounded like when I was buried deep inside her. I wanted to feel her nails in my back. I wanted to feel her tighten around me just before her body pulsated, grabbing my cock.

Normally, her painful shyness wouldn't be a turn on for me. I didn't, in my personal life, seek out the wallflowers. It wasn't that I didn't understand the male ego's urge to raise to the challenge, to make the reserved girl want me. I got it. I understood that. Once in a while, I felt that myself. But I also knew that when what I was looking for was just a fuck, I wasn't going to drag a girl like that through that kind of interaction. It would only reinforce her idea of her own worthlessness while at the same time bolstering her idea that men are pigs.

I didn't exactly have a type.

But whatever it was I went for... shy was not it.

Somehow, though, Ava's shyness was more than intriguing professionally. It was fucking adorable. Sweet. It made an unfamiliar surge of protectiveness swell up inside. There was a strong inner voice telling me to wrap her up and shelter her from the world.

Which was ridiculous.

Firstly because it was the absolute last thing she needed. What she needed was someone to take her by the hand and show her the world wasn't such a scary place.

But also, secondly, because that went against everything I believed about women. It went against everything I learned from the women I had dated: strong, independent, sexually confident women. Ava should have been embracing those attributes, not letting men protect her from them.

I sat through two more sessions that day- one housewife who was trying to overcome her husband's infidelity. It wasn't going well. While, professionally, I knew it was possible to come back from that kind of betrayal, I also knew that for many (if not most) it would never happen. There were some wounds that never healed. Or even if they did, they healed jagged, always reminding you of the imperfection. The next client was someone I had been seeing for years, a middle aged man who suffered with a crippling case of OCD. He, unlike the wife, was making slow but steady strides.

That was the job. The constant up and down. The wanting to do more, but knowing there was only so much you could do for them in one hour one day a week. They had to put in the work. They had to want and try to get better.

Knowing that didn't make it easier.

I rolled my shoulders as I made my way to the car, trying to shake off the work day, trying to clear it from my brain. I tried not to bring that shit home with me, to let it become something I obsessed about.

It was too easy to let that happen.

I made my way back to my apartment building, taking the elevator up to my floor and letting myself in.

My apartment was a testament to how far I had come in my life. From the tiny roach-infested apartment I had shared with my struggling mother, to the over-crowded foster homes I had been shuffled in and out of- dirty, loud, and uncomfortable as they had all been.

It was why I worked so hard: to make a life for myself that I could be proud of and comfortable in.

That was what my apartment meant to me. It was a nice place in a nice neighborhood with more space than I actually needed and professionally decorated. It was all dark wood floors and a deep cappuccino brown walls in the open floor plan living/dining/kitchen area. I walked over toward the windows, flipping open my stereo system and clicking through my play lists. I found one called "smoky blues" and heard Muddy Waters' voice fill the room. I walked over to the bar, pouring myself scotch neat and considering it for a moment before throwing it back.

Yeah. So I should have recused myself.

But I wasn't going to.

Partly because of selfish reasons.

But also because I could genuinely help her. I knew I could.

She deserved that. She deserved to have a normal life, a healthy sex life.

I squashed the tiny twinge of jealousy I felt at the idea of another man touching her. Because it was ridiculous.

Absolutely insane. That was the point of surrogacy, to get her comfortable with herself and her desires so she could go on and use that in her daily life. She could go on and enjoy sex. With other men.

I sighed, walking toward the bathroom and turning the water on cold.

Tuesday.

I had until then to get my fucking head in the game.

A part of me was pretty sure that would be nowhere near enough time.

First Session

The office was cleared for surrogate clients. First, because they generally took place later at night. Mostly, though, it was because it removed the strong sense of discomfort the client got at knowing that other people knew why they were there, what was going on beyond the office doors.

I was standing behind the desk looking over the next day's schedule when the door opened, bringing with it a wave of cold air. I felt my lips turning upward at the sight of her. She was dressed in black jeans, a black tank top, heels, and a wine colored sweater left open in the front. It was casual, but it was put together. Almost flirtatious. I had a distinct feeling it wasn't an outfit she had picked out herself.

"Ava," I breathed out her name.

"Dr. Hudson," she shot back, moving away from the door though she looked like she was ready to bolt.

"Chase," I corrected, walking out from behind the desk and making my way past her, toward the door. She stiffened when I got close, but didn't flinch away. I turned the lock on the door and moved to face her and said what was on my mind. "You look nice."

She almost immediately shook her head. "Oh, um... thanks," she fumbled, not holding my gaze.

My hand rose, pressing into her lower back. It was partly to steer her into my office, but it was also because I wanted to see how she reacted to the contact. She stiffened, but she didn't even attempt to move away. That was good. "You're welcome. How was your weekend?"

A look flashed over her face as she recalled the events, letting me know it wasn't exactly a great weekend for her. "Uneventful," she settled on, moving toward the alcove we had sat in during the introductory session.

"Ava," I said, holding an arm out, making it clear I wanted her to move toward me. "This way." She paused, but she walked toward me. I reached into the bookshelf, pulled a lever, and the hidden door clicked open. I kept my head turned toward her, watching for her reaction. I wasn't disappointed.

"Seriously?" she asked, her eyes wide, her brows raised. She looked dangerously close to laughing and I found myself wanting to know what that sounded like.

"Yup," I smiled, pressing into her lower back until she stepped through. I watched as her eyes skimmed the room. She took in the seating area to the side, the stereo, the decanters of liquor, the bed. They widened a bit when they landed there. "Why don't you find some music to put on?" I suggested, waving toward the stereo, trying to get her attention away from the bed.

I offered her a drink and she accepted red wine, putting on a coffeehouse playlist. It was the least likely to be confused with something sexual on the list of choices.

"How about we go sit down?" I suggested, waving a hand toward the sectional in the corner. I turned my back on her, giving her a minute to settle in as I turned on the fireplace.

I turned to find she had seated herself as far away from where I had set my wineglass down as possible. I drank my wine, giving her a second, then sat down near her, my feet touching hers but my hips pivoted away. My arm was thrown across the back cushions, but not touching her. "Nervous?" I asked, my free hand moving to land on her knee.

Her head bobbed slightly. "Yes."

"What exactly are you nervous about? Me touching you?" She nodded, looking down at my hand. "I'm touching you right now. Do you want me to stop?" I asked, hoping she wasn't already at the point of retreat as I squeezed her knee softly.

She paused, mulling it over, before deciding, "No."

"Good. Because I don't want to stop."

Hell, I didn't want to stop until I was buried deep inside her, my teeth nipping into her lower lip as I swallowed her moans.

"Wh..." she started, then changed her mind. "Okay."

My hand moved down from her knee, stroking down the front of her leg, then moving back up. It was chaste, but I could tell by the jolt through her body that she wasn't seeing it that way.

Her wineglass was empty and I took it, getting rid of it, before moving back to her, placing my hand on the knee further from me, caging her in.

That was when she started freaking out.

Her eyes went wide, her breath got caught in her chest, her body went ramrod straight.

"Ava," I broke in and her head snapped in my direction. "Breathe," I reminded her. She sucked in a breath and exhaled it slowly. "Good. Now, tell me why you're anxious."

"I feel trapped."

"Okay." I looked to where my arm was blocking her in then squeezed her knee. "Are you really trapped?" I asked, knowing that it didn't matter if she actually was or wasn't. That wasn't how anxiety worked. It couldn't be reasoned with.

"No."

"Can you leave at any time?"

"Yes."

I went for the jugular. "Do you think I would be mad or disappointed if you needed to get up and walk away?" There was the flash of panic, the proof of my guess.

Her eyes went up to mine for a second, considering me. "No."

"Okay so why don't we stop thinking about that?" I suggested, my hand going down the front of her leg, moving around the calf, then settling back onto her knee. "Do you like this?" I asked, my fingers brushing up her thigh.

Her eyes fell from mine but not before I saw the spark there. It was just a fizzle really, but it was there. Desire.

"Yes," she admitted.

"Good. I like that. I like touching you," I admitted, letting the arm that was draped across the back of the couch slip downward, settling behind her back but not wrapping around her, not wanting to actually trap her. She straightened slightly and I scooted my hips closer so we were side by side. "And I'm not just saying that because it's my job."

But I fucking should have been. Not even halfway into our first session and I was blurring lines. Not good. I needed to rein it in.

Then, "Really?" she asked, sounding almost... hopeful as a bright red blush crept up into her cheeks.

Shit.

My hand moved from her leg to start stroking across her jaw then gently grabbing her chin, forcing her to look at me. "Babe if I saw you in a bar, I'd have taken you home in a heartbeat." It was the truth. I saw her, looking all gorgeous and uncertain sitting in some bar, I'd have made a beeline for her. It was as simple as that.

Her gaze fell from mine immediately, looking like she was struggling with whether to put her faith to rest in my words or not. The silence hung, my fingers still holding her chin, waiting for her gaze to rise again. When her brown eyes found mine, I asked, "Do you believe me?"

"Yes," she decided, her voice sure.

I felt myself nod, my hand still holding her face, leaning in slightly. "I would have walked over to you, gotten close, whispered in your ear, told you how fucking gorgeous you are..." Her eyes widened, but I plowed on, digging myself in further. "And then I would bring you back to my apartment and as soon as you stepped inside, I would push you up hard against the door and crush my lips to yours." My thumb moved out, stroking across the lips in question, my eyes watching the motion. Her lips parted slightly. Her body shifted as she pressed her thighs closer together. *Fuck me.* "Does that sound good?" I asked, my thumb making another swipe, slipping into the crease slightly.

"Y... yes," she admitted, swallowing hard.

"Are you turned on, Ava?" I asked, knowing my answer, but needing to hear her say it.

There was barely even a pause before, "Yes."

I felt the growl in the back of my throat, more turned on than I thought I would be. I was more turned on than I had ever been in a professional setting. I had barely fucking touched her. "I like that," I admitted, my hand sliding from her chin, across her jaw, then down her neck. She shivered. *Fucking shivered.* I felt myself chuckle slightly. "You're so sensitive."

"Not usually," she said, forcing the words out like they cost her to admit.

Fuck me. Not usually. That meant it was something special with me. My head tilted toward hers, my nose grazing her jaw. "Just for me then?" I asked and her head fell slightly backward, unconsciously giving me more access.

"I guess," she whispered.

They shouldn't have, but those words felt good. Way too good.

"Do you want me to kiss you here?" I asked, my nose brushing under her ear.

Another barely-there pause. "Yes."

"Tell me," I demanded, needing to hear her say it. Not as her doctor or surrogate. Just as a man. I needed to hear it.

There was another body shiver. "Tell you what?" she hedged, knowing damn well what I wanted.

"Tell me you want me to kiss your neck," I clarified.

And that's when she tensed up. Her body went rigid. Her breathing got too fast. She was anxious. "Ava," I started, tilting my head up to look at her. She swallowed hard as she looked down at me and shook her head. "No you don't want me to? Or no you can't ask?" I pressed, trying to force back the desire and be there for what she needed. But, fuck, I was praying it wasn't the former.

"I can't ask," she said, her voice a croaking sound.

I fought back the surge of pleasure at that admission and shrugged. "Okay. We can work on the verbal stuff," I told her neck, turning my attention back to it. "But first... this..."

I let my lips press in softly, feeling her body jolt, seeing her hand slam down on her leg. Surprised? Sure. But more so, excited. She was responding. My lips pressed in harder, a hint of teeth against her skin, before my tongue moved outward and traced down her neck. My hand on the side of her neck curled in slightly as her head tilted, giving me more access. I let my mouth move down toward her collarbone before I forced myself to stop. To pull back. It was too much, too fast. If I pushed, she would dart. And she wouldn't come back.

I lifted my head and let my hands float back into her soft hair. "Open your eyes." She struggled in a breath, forcing her eyes open, and slowly lifted her gaze to mine. "Good girl," I murmured, inwardly wincing. She wasn't a random chick at a bar. I couldn't fucking talk to her like that. God damn it. "Did you enjoy that?" I asked, forcing my tone to be normal. Or as close to normal as possible when all I wanted to do was run my lips and tongue over every inch of her until she was moaning my name.

"Yes," she said softly, shaking me out of my fantasy.

"What do you want now?" I asked, trying to veer us back into the session, trying to get her more comfortable with talking to me.

26

Her eyes went huge, looking panicked.

"Let's try this again," I said, smiling a little. "Do you want me to keep kissing your neck?" I asked, leaning down and placing a feather-light kiss to her neck. As light a touch as it was, it sent a jolt through her body. "Or do you want to try something else for a while?"

"Something else," she said, her words barely audible.

And fuck, that was what I wanted to hear.

"Okay. How about you turn around?" I suggested.

"Why?" she asked immediately, her body going stiff.

Interesting.

She was calmer, less anxious when I was closer to her, when I was touching her. Free of that, her anxiety settled right back in.

Which went completely against everything she had told me in the introductory meeting. And what I read in her questionnaire.

Very interesting.

"Because," I said, my hand moving to stroke down her arm, "I am going to give you a massage."

"Oh," she said, her gaze moving from me and toward the bed.

"Do you think you would like that?" I asked and felt her shrug. "Okay. Let's find out then," I said, moving away from her so she had room to turn her back to me.

There was the briefest of pauses before she turned. Not wanting to give her any time to get anxious, my hands went right to her shoulders, all twisted into knots. Within seconds, Ava was gone. Off somewhere else. Lost in her own head. It was in the stiffness in her body and the way she didn't react whatsoever to my hands on her. "Where are you? You're not with me."

"Sorry," she mumbled. Knee-jerk, like it tripped off her tongue constantly.

"Don't be sorry. Tell me what you were thinking about."

"My roommate."

27

"Why?"

"He's a massage therapist."

He. Her roommate was a he. I felt a rush of something weird. Foreign. It was a swirling, uncomfortable sensation in my chest and stomach.

Jesus Christ.

Jealousy.

What the hell was wrong with me?

"Ah. I see. Have you ever let him give you a massage?"

"What do you think?" she asked on a half-laugh, half-snort.

I felt myself chuckle, working my hands up into her sore muscles. "Why don't you tell me about him?"

"Why?"

"Because you are having communication issues. I figure your roommate is a safe enough topic to get started." And also, I just wanted to know more about the man she let share her life. Because that was what she did. Whether she realized it or not, she shared her life with him. I was curious to see why he was different. I wanted to know why he was allowed in when all other men were kept at a distance.

"He's an asshole," she said easily, laughing.

Interesting. "Why is he an asshole?"

"He teases me all the time," she told me, a bit of bitterness rising into her voice.

"What does he tease you about?"

"The way I dress." There was nothing wrong with the way she dressed. Understated. Casual, but put together. She pulled it off. It didn't exactly scream "take me", but it suited her. "How I am uptight and a little OCD about things being clean. About my needing to get laid."

She was right. He was an asshole.

"He sounds like a good guy," I drawled and she giggled.

"He's actually not a bad guy all in all. It's just like... living with a teenage boy. He's a slob and has wild parties all the time." It was right then that I had their relationship pegged.

The jealousy vanished (as absurd as it was that it existed at all in the first place). Ava and her roommate had an adult brother/sister type of bond. He drove her nuts by being a dick, but she loved him regardless. He, I was sure just by knowing her for the matter of a few hours, loved her as well. He just was too immature to show it. "Oh, and then there's the ear-piercing screams..." she went on.

"Screams?" I asked, my hands pausing by her hips.

"Yes," she said, sounding shy. "From... women."

"Ah," I said, smiling because she couldn't see me. "Does that make you uncomfortable?"

"Only when I have to wake up in the morning and explain to said women that Jake is gone, he won't call, and they'll never see him again," she said in a way that suggested it was something she had to do frequently.

"Do you think that has had any effect on how you view sex?"

"Not really. Except knowing with absolute certainty that I don't want to do it with him."

That was what I wanted to hear.

And she had come out of her shell to share a little.

So I could move on.

"Does this feel good?" I asked as her head moved to the side so my hands could work her shoulders.

"Yes," she said, her tone a little airy.

Fuck if the sound didn't send a stab of desire through my system.

"Good," I said, brushing her soft hair to one side of her neck so my lips could press down into her skin again. "Why don't you turn back around?" I asked, nipping into her earlobe.

"Okay," she agreed, her tone even more breathy.

She turned and almost instantaneously, her eyes lost focus. Her body went rigid. She was remembering something from her past. Something that made her look both anxious and incredibly sad at the same time.

29

"Come back to me," I said, watching as her gaze moved up to mine and the blurriness subsided. "What were you just thinking about?"

Her eyes dropped from mine, watching the collar of my shirt like it just became the most fascinating thing in the world.

"The last time someone kissed me."

My hand went up to her face, stroking her cheek, wanting to wipe away the look of mortification there. "Tell me about it." The panic rose up quick and strong. "You have to put the work in, Ava," I reminded her.

Her teeth bit into the inside of her cheek for a second as her eyes dropped. But she started talking. "Jake was having a party. There was a guy who... took interest in me..."

"Just one?" I asked, smiling, not able to help myself.

Her brows drew together slightly. "Yes. Just one. And he just... didn't seem deterred by my lack of enthusiasm. Then, hours later, he finally leaned in and..."

"And what happened?" I pried, knowing she was just going to let it hang there if I didn't force her to say more.

"I handled it for a few seconds then freaked and ran."

"Hmm," I said, my other hand going to her face, cradling it. "What did he say?"

"I never saw him again."

Jesus Christ.

He just... let her freak out and run and didn't even try to figure out what happened? I knew my fellow men were clueless, but fuck... who would pass up on a chance to get with her? Even if it required a little work?

"A face like this, babe, he should have been bringing you flowers and jewelry and chocolate until you got comfortable with him and let him try again." I paused, watching the flush take over her features. "Do you have any idea what men would do to possess beauty like this? And here I am, holding it." Now if only she wasn't my client... "Tell me you want me to kiss you." She needed to say it. I needed to feel her. Taste her. "Ava, tell me."

I watched as she slowly licked her lips. "I want you to kiss me," she said on a whisper.

"Thank god," I groaned, leaning in, grabbing her face, and pressed my lips to hers. It was firm, but gentle, not wanting to scare her with the intensity of my desire. A current moved through her body on a soft moan and her lips started responding, begging for more. My head tilted, my arm going around her back, deepening the kiss.

I got maybe a minute in before her lips went lax against mine. Her body was stiff. She was completely checked out. She didn't so much as open her eyes when I stopped kissing her and moved away.

"Ava," I said and her eyes shot open, looking shocked. "On a scale of one to ten, how bad is the anxiety?"

"Six or seven," she said, her hand moving up to close over her throat, like she was trying to break down the barrier that wouldn't let her breathe right.

"Okay," I said, moving away to sit back on the couch. "Come here."

"What?" she asked, taking slow, deep breaths.

"It hasn't exactly escaped my notice that I have been touching you and you have yet to put a finger on me. Come here," I said, holding an arm out. "Put your head on my chest." Her eyes, already big, got bigger. Her hand closed over her throat hard. "At least try, Ava," I coaxed.

Then she nodded a little and moved over toward me. Her body pressed against mine hesitantly and there was a long moment where I was sure she was going to back away before she finally scooted in and rested her head against my chest. I let her have a moment to adjust, to get comfortable, before my arm went around her. "You okay?"

"Yeah."

"What's the level?" I asked though from her steady breathing and her soft body, I knew she was nowhere near a six or a seven anymore.

"Four?" she half-asked, half-declared.

"Be proud of the little victories, Ava," I said, taking my other arm and pulling her hand into mine, interlocking our fingers.

When she didn't fight it, didn't struggle, in fact, settled in more, I started stroking my hand up and down her back slowly, enjoying the feel of her relaxing. It wasn't long, maybe ten minutes passed at most before I felt her body completely sigh into me, a small murmuring sound coming out of her lips as she fell asleep.

She fell asleep.

On me.

She trusted me. Already. Therapeutically, that was great. But also, it was just nice in general. It was painfully obvious that she didn't trust anyone. But she trusted me. And all it took was two hours of knowing me.

She woke up a bit freaked a while later, pushing off of me, trying to shrug back into her shields. Then, voice shaky and weak, she asked what the next session was.

The next session was something I had tried really hard to not focus on while she was with me. That was because the next session involved the both of us taking our clothes off. I was hard enough just having her near me, kissing me, laying on my chest. I didn't need to think about her doing those things while naked- those fantastic fucking legs wrapped around me... her breasts pressing against my chest... her nipples...

Okay. Enough.

I explained, soothing over her fears, reminding her to be in the moment, not worried about the future. Then I walked her to her car.

I unlocked the door to her little hatchback, watching her shuffle her feet, awkwardly thanking me for walking her.

And I couldn't, or didn't want, to fight it anymore.

"We're outside the office," I said, running a hand through my hair. "I'm not supposed to do this..." I was talking more to myself than her, but when I saw her brows draw slightly together, I knew it was useless. "Fuck it," I growled and my lips crashed onto hers.

It was hard. Demanding. It was full of all the repressed desire I had been trying to keep a rein on. First, because it wasn't professional. Second, because I didn't want to scare her.

But apparently that was not a concern. With my lips insistent on hers, her body came alive. It sparked like electricity. And all I wanted to do was...

"Fuck," I growled, pushing away from her, running a hand across my brow. Fuck fuck fuck. "Sorry," I said, taking a deep breath as I reached out toward her, stroking my thumb across her chin and lips where she had the slightest trace of beard burn marring her flawless skin. "That wasn't exactly professional of me, huh?" I asked, shaking my head at myself.

"It's okay," she said, swallowing hard, her face still flushed with desire.

"You touched me," I told her.

"What?"

"You touched me. When I kissed you. Without being told or asked to. You just did it." Her eyes went surprised, but there was a little light of pride there too and I felt myself smiling at her. "Baby steps, but that's really good, Ava." I reached behind her, grabbing the door handle and pulling it open. I needed her to go. I needed to get my head together. "I'll see you Thursday," I told her, watching her lower into her car. I pushed the door closed, murmuring to myself, "I'm looking forward to it."

Because, fuck, I was.

And that was a problem.

After the Session

I went home frustrated. No surprise there. Sexually. Emotionally. Professionally. Pretty little Ava Davis was creating all kinds of problems. Problems that I should have been walking away from.

I slammed the door to my apartment a bit too hard, pulling at my tie until it loosened enough for me to feel like I could breathe, moving over toward the couch in the living room and lying down, hand over my head.

Things were finally in place. My psychology practice was steady and stable. My loans were paid back. I had a nice place to live. I had good friends. Life was going the way I worked and studied my ass off to make it go. All those all nighters in college. All the empty coffee cups. All the parties I missed. All the years scrounging up every spare penny I could to pay the student loans. It was all to bring me to where I was. Personally and professionally.

Apparently all it took to throw things into chaos was a blonde haired, brown eyed wallflower with the sweetest little honey voice and a heady cocktail of insecurities and anxieties.

I sighed, shaking my head at myself, letting the last few sleepless nights catch up to me as I drifted off.

———

"Mom?" I called, walking in from school, my little six year old thumbs tucked into the straps of my backpack at my shoulders.

The other kids didn't get to walk home alone. Not yet. Their parents said they were too young. It was too far. Bad things could happen to them. I felt really grown up to be the only one who was allowed to walk themselves home. It didn't even occur to me that it was weird that my mom didn't come to pick-up and get me even though she was home.

Besides, we didn't have a backyard so the walk home was the only time I got to be outside all day except for recess at school. I liked it.

The house was smoky. I knew from the assembly at school that smoking was bad for you. I tried to tell Mom that when I came home, but she waved her hand at me and told me that they calmed her down when she didn't feel good. So I didn't think they could be all that bad if they made her feel better.

But the smoke always made me cough a little and I shrugged out of my backpack and propped the front door open so the smoke would clear.

"Mom?" I called again, walking in through the apartment, my dirty clothes tossed into a piled in a corner, ashtrays overflowing on the coffee table.

In the kitchen, one of her special bottles was laying on the dining room table. One of the special bottles which were full of the drinks that smelled bad enough to make my eyes water. Mom liked those too. Like her cigarettes, they made her calm too.

The bottle was almost empty and I figured she must have gone down the street to get more from the store.

So I did my homework. Then I looked around for something to eat.

The fridge was empty. But that was normal. Maybe if she picked up more of her special bottles, she would pick up some food for dinner too.

I went to bed still hoping for that, belly growling and churning angrily.

But that was normal too.

School would feed me breakfast and lunch the next day. Then my belly would feel better.

I heard the slam sometime later, waking me out of a dead sleep and making me shoot up in bed, my heart pounding in my chest.

"Ow," Mom's voice groaned and I flew out of bed, moving out into the living room to find her half-sprawled across the living room floor, rubbing at her ankle. "Oh, hey Chasey baby," she said, smiling up at me, her eyes glassy.

"Hi Mom," I said, sitting down next to her, noticing there was a tear up the side of her dress. "You okay?"

That was all it took.

A simple question.

A normal question to ask someone who had just tripped.

But a question like that, for my mother, well... it meant more.

I knew this because she burst into tears. Not the quiet type. The loud, sobbing, hysterical type. She laid down fully, her forehead to the floor, her entire body wrecking with her cries as she pounded her fist against the floor. The cries turned into a sort of screeching that had me bringing my hands up to my ears to try to block it out, rocking and humming to myself.

That was how the cops found us a while later. Me rocking and humming. Mom crying and screaming.

Then the cops took me into the kitchen and talked to me. Then other people showed up.

They told my mom that she couldn't take care of me anymore. At least until she was feeling better.

Then they took me away.

And suddenly it wasn't just my mom who was crying and screaming.

It was me too.

—

"Fuck," I growled, sitting up on the couch, holding my head in my hands. It was nothing new. The nightmares that weren't nightmares, they were memories. They weren't new. I couldn't sleep without at least one of them coming back. And, believe me, there were plenty to choose from.

It had been a long time since it was that one, though. The first one. The one that started them all. The one that cut the deepest.

Months. It had been months since it was that one.

I stood up, grabbing my keys, and charging out of my apartment. I didn't want to be alone with my ghosts. Not when they were breathing down my neck, forcing me to acknowledge them.

It was the stress.

I knew that.

Stress brought them back worse.

And I was stressed about the whole Ava situation.

So I walked out of my building and across the street, bent on getting a drink or two, maybe some dinner, before heading back home to pass out.

That was, until I opened the door, and froze.

Because there she was. Ava, sitting at the bar with a martini and an appetizer plate. She seemed uncomfortable and alone. In *my* bar. The bar across from *my* apartment building.

Fuck me.

And, again, there really wasn't a choice. I knew I was supposed to walk away. Leave. To do anything but what I ended up doing. I went to her. I sat down with her. I talked to her. I figured out why she was there.

Then the asshole walked up.

The roommate.

The one who dragged her to the bar in the first place then abandoned her.

"Hey. Don't bother, dude. She's not interested." I felt myself almost start to nod, glad that she had someone in her life to fend off unwanted guys at bars. But, unfortunately, Jake wasn't done speaking. "She's not interested in anyone but her sex doctor."

The look of absolute horror that came across Ava's face was enough to make me want to drag the dick outside and give him a different kind of talking-to.

But that wasn't my place.

"Shut the hell up, Jake," Ava demanded, her eyes begging him to follow her orders.

But apparently Jake was dense or drunk or a dick. Or all three. He just kept going. "No seriously. She's like... frigid dude. You don't want her."

Jesus Christ.

Ava's gaze flew to her lap where she was wringing her hands together, a blush over her cheeks, her teeth nipping into her lower lip. She looked like she wanted the ground to open up and swallow her right then and there.

I sighed, leaning in front of her, extending my hand to her asshole roommate. "Dr. Chase Hudson," I said, watching Jake stiffen.

"Oh," he said, dropping my hand.

38

"Yeah... *oh*," I enunciated, fighting hard against the anger in my system as I glanced at Ava again. "What you just did to her is absolutely fucking unacceptable," I growled.

"Dude, I didn't mean any offense..."

"It's not me you should be apologizing to, it's her. Do you have any idea how insensitive that was? Knowing that she is struggling , to rub it in her face in front of someone you thought was a stranger? You need to take better care of her."

Didn't he see how lucky he was to be in her life? To share her bumbling, awkward, stumbling speech? To get to see her shy smiles? To hear her laugh?

"I'm not her boyfriend or brother man," Jake insisted, looking uncomfortable. But he was just pressing the issue to save his pride. He felt bad. And that was good. He should.

"No, but you're the reason she's here in the first place. This obviously isn't the kind of thing she's comfortable with. And then you fucking abandon her. Then make fun of her? Who does shit like that? She's in your life. You care about her at all... fucking do better," I said, throwing some money on the bar, too pissed to stick around and hear any kind of excuses he might come with.

I took a breath, turning back to Ava. "Ava," I said, my tone softer as I waited for her gaze to find mine. When it did, I offered her a small smile. "I will see you Thursday," I said, turning and making my way back across the street.

Thursday.

How the fuck was I going to get myself under control by Thursday?

Second Session

Thursday was a blur of patients. The wife again. There was still no progress. If anything, the bitterness was getting worse- poisoning the well of potential reconciliation. I had the distinct impression I would be helping her through her divorce before the end of the year.

Such was the job sometimes.

I was looking over some notes when the door swung open, bringing a rush of cold air that made my gaze rise.

And there she was.

And she looked beautiful.

Like herself, but not.

She was dressed up. She wore a form-fitting black long sleeve dress, stockings, and heels. "Ava," I breathed out her name, dropping the papers. "Can you lock the door behind you please?" I asked, attempting a casual tone as she turned to do so. Before she even turned back, I was across the room. And then it just... tripped out. "You look beautiful." As would be expected, my clumsy compliment was met with silence. I sighed inwardly, shaking my head. "Come on, let's go get you a drink, okay?" I asked, sensing the anxiety coming off her in waves.

Not surprising.

Getting naked with someone new was usually anxiety inducing. For someone who struggled with intimacy... even more so. And for someone who was paying someone else to help them get over those hangups? I couldn't imagine.

I got her a martini. She put on music. Singer-songwriters because it was a safe bet. Non-sexual.

"Why don't you kick out of those shoes?" I suggested after I led her over toward the sectional and went to turn on the fireplace.

Then I turned and sat down next to her, giving her no space to pull into herself, no time to freak out, as I wrapped an arm behind her back and pulled her legs over my lap.

"Hi," I said, tilting my head down at her.

"Hi," she said back on a whisper, a charming little lopsided smile on her face.

Sometimes it wasn't the massive flirting, the outlandish confidence, the alluring sexual prowess. Sometimes all it took was a woman being fully, unapologetically... herself. Even if that woman was shy and awkward and unsure of herself. That was what got a man's attention- genuineness.

And every fucking thing about Ava was real.

And it was becoming a problem for me.

I dropped my eyes from hers, my hand going to run down her hip and thigh, the silky smoothness of her stockings gliding across my palm. "I like these," I admitted. "Did you wear them for me?"

There was a strange lightness in her eyes at that, something passing behind them and I found myself wanting to know what it was. But then her gaze dropped to watch my hand and she answered her lap. "Yes."

Fuck me.

"You're so sweet," I said, unable to hold out any longer and I leaned down and started planting small kisses across her

41

jaw- her skin smelling like her. Something soft and feminine. Vanilla. Lotion or perfume. It was practically fucking narcotic. Her eyes closed on a small sigh. "Ava..."

"Yeah?" she asked, her eyes still closed.

"Kiss me."

Her eyes flew open, looking more surprised than horrified though and I figured that was a good sign. Her gaze lowered to my lips and I fought the smile I felt forming. She wanted me. It wasn't just because she knew she was supposed to be intimate with me. It wasn't something she had to talk herself into. She just... wanted me.

Her arm lifted tentatively off her leg, hovering in the air for the barest of seconds then brushing across the side of my face before settling at the back of my neck. I closed my eyes, taking a steadying breath, trying to force down the urgency of my desire. She needed patience and understanding. She needed me to get a fucking hold of myself.

My eyes opened to find her watching me. Then she tilted upward and closed the space between us, her lips falling on mine softly. Carefully.

But the contact sent off shock waves to my system. My arm around her shoulders tightened, my fingers dug into her shoulder, trying to let her have the control she needed. Then her lips pressed the kiss deeper and, fuck me, she dug her teeth into my lower lip.

I could only take so much.

I grabbed her and pulled her across me until she was straddling my waist. Her hands went up, cradling my face, completely lost in the moment. In the sensations. Her tongue slipped between my lips and my hands crushed into her hips- equally trying to pull her closer and keep her at a distance. Her arms went around my neck, her hips sinking down.

There was nothing else in the world in that moment.

I could have let her kiss me forever.

But we had a session.

And I wasn't exactly unhappy to end the kiss so I could see more of her. All of her.

My hands went to the sides of her face, guiding her backward, watching as her eyes slowly fluttered open. Heavy lidded. Full of longing. "Jesus Christ you're beautiful," I murmured, in the moment too far gone to think about my professional boundaries. My finger traced across her cheekbone. "I want to see more of you," I started, watching as the desire drained from her brown eyes. "Take off your dress, sweetheart." Her body went rigid. Fuck. "Don't freak out," I said softly, my hands moving to her hips and scrunching into the material so I didn't start pulling it off her. "I want to take this off you so badly, but you need to be the one to do it." Unfortunately. "Please take it off for me."

I could see a dozen thoughts floating across her face, stifling a smile because I knew how highly people with anxiety prized their ability to not be obvious about it, to not let other people see they were struggling. But fuck if her eyes weren't an open book. She had the worst poker face in the world.

Her hands moved down her body to settle on top of mine, squeezing, silently telling me to let go. So I did. She took a few deep breaths before grabbing the hem of her dress and quickly (before she could talk herself out of it) ripped the material off and tossed it to the side.

"*Fuck me*," I heard myself growl, thankful she was holding her hips off of mine or she would have felt how much of an effect she was having on me.

Because, make no mistake, there was nothing fucking professional about how I was feeling right then- about how I was looking at her- about how much I wanted her.

She had on a black lacy bra with matching panties and garter belt, the black stockings clasped high up on her thighs. It was a lingerie set meant to drive a man to distraction.

She accomplished that task.

But it wasn't just the lingerie. It was her. Ava. The woman underneath the lace. Her collarbones, the breasts above

43

the cups of her bra, her flat though not toned tummy, the flare of hips. Fuck... even the tiny iridescent spiderweb lines of stretch marks over said hips. Just... perfect. And I wasn't even going to get started on her legs.

"Was this for me too?" I asked of her lingerie, watching as she nodded and gave me a shy smile. "Baby, stand up," I coaxed, pressing into her knees until she moved off of me to stand. My hands rested at the tops of her thigh-highs.

"I... ah..." Oh, *fuck me*... the stammering. I couldn't take it. She was too sweet. "Wanted to say thank you."

"Babe, what do you have to thank me for?" I asked, watching her face.

"Because... because you're helping me so much."

Jesus.

"Oh, babe," I said, leaning forward and resting my forehead against her stomach. "You're so perfect." Slowly, her hand came down to rest on the top of my head and I twisted slightly to plant a kiss on her belly. My gaze found hers again and I had nothing to say. There were no words. I always had the words. That was my job. To talk to people. Christ. "Well... you're welcome," I went with finally, smiling clumsily up at her.

Caught off guard, she fucking... giggled. *Giggled.* The sound sent a warmth through my system and I felt my smile stretch wide enough to make my cheeks hurt.

I reached out, pressing her backward so I could stand then quickly shrugged out of my jacket and made quirk work of my shirt buttons. Her eyes stayed stubbornly on mine. "Ava look. I want you to look." I watched her as she watched me, tossing my shirt aside and moving my hands to the buttons of my slacks. She watched until the pants were gone, her gaze going back up to my face. She was getting nervous. "What do you want to do?" I asked.

I expected a head shake, a confused look, a stammered reply.

44

The absolute last thing I could have prepared for was her closing the space between us, her arms wrapping around my back, and her head moving to rest underneath my chin. I felt my body go stiff for the barest of seconds, too surprised to move, before my arms went around her, crushing her to me.

"I'd like to stay like this all night too baby," I said. Because I did. I could have walked us toward the bed, curled us both onto our sides, and held her. Happily. Until morning. But that was the problem. I needed to get it together. I needed to get my head in the game. "But it's time."

"It's time for what?" she asked, sounding almost half asleep. And then, fuck, she turned her head and *kissed my chest*.

"It's time to take the rest of our clothes off," I said and she went still. "Don't stiffen up. It's okay. You can take as much time as you need, okay?"

"Okay," she said, sounding like it was anything but okay.

"Do you want me to finish first?" I asked, watching as her eyes went over my body, stopping just above the waist of my boxer briefs. "Ava?"

Her eyes flew back up guiltily and she croaked out, "Me."

I nodded, turning, sitting back down on the sectional, watching her. "Ava," I said, my voice a little harsh, trying to grab her attention. "Why don't you start with the stockings, okay?"

Then she did. She unclasped the garter and slid the material down her long (perfect) legs. I bit the inside of my cheek at seeing how badly her hands were shaking. I knew it was hard for her. I also knew that she had to push herself or the therapy would go nowhere. Then she made faster work of the garter. Just the bra and panties were left. Two small swatches of fabric and I could see her completely. She bent forward, her hair cascading forward, offering her a small amount of privacy I couldn't begrudge her as she reached behind her back and let her bra fall to the ground. Her hands slipped down and hooked into her panties. Then she was out of them too.

But I couldn't drink in the view. I couldn't soak up the image of her.

Because the second she was out of her clothes, she lost it.

"I can't. I can't," she said, her voice dangerously close to tears as she went to the floor, pulling her legs to her chest, blocking her nudity from me. "I can't. I'm sorry. I just..." her body started rocking back and forth, trying to comfort herself and I felt like the biggest shit in the world.

I moved down behind her, legs going out on her sides. "Okay. It's okay," I said, reaching for her, praying she wouldn't shy away. She didn't. I pulled her to me until the side of her face was against my chest. My arms went around her and I pressed a kiss on the top of her head. Like an apology. "It's alright, Ava. Take a breath, okay?" I urged, her body not having inhaled at all since I got behind her, which only succeeded in allowing her anxiety to spike. She followed instructions. "Good. Again," I said, my hands moving into her soft hair and stroking it. "Give me a number."

"Eight."

Fuck. Eight.

"Okay. Keep breathing. What do you need from me right now?"

There was a long pause. "I need you to rub my back."

I shifted so I could reach her and stroked my fingers up and down her spine. "Like this?"

I could practically feel the tension draining out of her. "Yes."

So then I stroked her back. Until she was languid and calm against me. Until she was at the point where she was still naked, but not freaking out about it.

"Okay," I said, my hands moving across her back and under her knees to lift her. "I am going to take you to the bed." Immediately, her body got tense. "No, don't tense up," I said

46

gently. "I told you there isn't going to be any sexual contact today. Okay? Do you trust me?"

The was barely even a pause before she answered. "Yes."

And damn if that didn't feel good.

She trusted me. Without even having to think about it. This girl who didn't seem to trust anyone... trusted me.

"Okay. I am going to let you get under the covers so we can do this slowly. So we don't have another panic attack. That was my fault."

"It wasn't..."

"Yes, it was," I cut her off, not letting her have more than a second to think it was her. It wasn't. I fucked up. "I shouldn't have sat back like you were about to put on a show for me. That wasn't a good move. I should have known better." I *did* know better. Which only made it worse. If I was just some clueless asshole she met, I'd have an excuse. As it was, I had none.

I pulled back the comforter and let her slide under, pulling the blankets up to her shoulders. She held it in place but scooted toward the center of the bed, giving me space to climb in beside her.

"I am going to take my boxers off," I told her, reaching for the material.

"Okay."

My head tilted with how quickly she accepted that, not sounding anxious at all suddenly. "Do you want to watch?" Beneath the sheets, her legs shifted. And I knew. I just knew she was pressing them together because she was turned on. Jesus. She nodded slightly. "That's so hot babe," I said honestly, pushing down the boxers and stepping out of them. I gave her a moment to look. And she did, a slight blush creeping up in her cheeks, but she didn't look away. Then I climbed in underneath the sheets with her. "What are you thinking?"

We both turned onto our sides facing each other, but she brought her knees up toward her chest as a barrier.

"Ava, tell me baby. You can trust me, remember?" My hand moved out and rested on her cheek. "Please."

"I was thinking about you..." she trailed off and the blush went bright red, her gaze fell. Like she couldn't face me and admit whatever it was that was in her head. "Inside me."

Fuck me.

Okay.

I let my eyes close for a minute, trying to pull forward some more self-control. "God, babe, that makes me happy. You have no idea how badly I want to be inside you." Like never before, honestly. I'd wanted a lot of women before. I'd had a lot of women before. But not one made me want her like I wanted Ava that moment with her shy little admission that to her actually meant the world. She wanted me inside her. She never wanted anyone inside her.

"I have some idea," she mumbled, biting into her lip, her gaze shifting downward.

I choked on my laugh for a second before it burst from my chest, a surprised and appreciative sound. I hadn't expected that from her. It was cheeky and funny and it insinuated something sexual. She had a lot more to her than she let people see. But she was letting me peek at it. I had a weird, sneaky voice whisper that I was never going to be satisfied until I saw it all. "You're pretty amazing, do you know that?"

Something I couldn't place came over her face before she looked away. "Okay. What now?"

"Touch me," I said simply. That got her attention. It also got me an eyebrow raise. "You want to, don't you?" I asked, turning onto my back. "Here," I said, "I'll give you more access."

A small smile toyed at her lips. "Are you like... being playful?" she asked, her brows drawing together.

"I'm not always serious you know," I said, turning my head on my pillow to look at her. I found myself wanting her to know about the me that I was outside of the office, outside of the mask I had to wear for the sake of professionalism.

48

"Good to know," she said, moving herself upward as her hand hovered over my skin for an excruciatingly long moment before lowering down onto my chest. Her hand shifted to the center of my chest, moving downward and I heard my breath hiss out of my mouth. The sound apparently emboldened her as her palm moved over my skin greedily, hungrily.

"So my nudity is okay," I observed, needing to take some of my focus off what her hand was doing to me.

"I guess," she said and her hand stilled.

"Okay," I said, kicking the covers off my body, letting myself be completely exposed, watching her face for a reaction. Expecting hesitation. Fear. Anxiety. But, no. What I saw was pure... heat.

"Can I see more of you now?" I asked, pushing up onto my elbow on my side so I could look at her.

There was a long hesitation before, "Okay."

I took a deep breath, trying to calm the urgency I felt, forcing myself to go slow. My hand went down to her feet, slowly exposing her long legs. "These are great legs," I said, stroking my hand over them.

"Thank you."

There wasn't even a pause. "You're getting better at that."

"Well you won't stop feeding compliments to me," she shrugged, trying to brush it off.

"Hey," I said, my tone a little too rough. "I don't want you thinking I am just saying shit to say it. When I tell you how beautiful you are, I mean it. I want you to know that. And I want you to start believing it too." Shit. That was a little harsh. A little too... demanding. She didn't need me to be an alpha asshole when she was trying to trip her way through gaining some confidence.

"I... believe you," she mumbled.

"Do *you* believe it?" I pressed.

"I'm getting there," she allowed.

"Progress," I said, smiling a little.

"Yeah," she agreed.

My hand went to the sheets and pulled them, exposing her fully from the waist down. Immediately, her thighs snapped together, blocking her pussy from view. "Your choice?" I asked, my hand pressing down at the lowest point of her belly, forcing myself to keep it a safe distance from her heat. "Or what you thought I wanted?" I asked.

Her brows scrunched up. "What?"

"Completely shaving," I supplied, looking at the pale, flawless skin, but not able to see anything really.

"What? Did you expect everything to be all... unruly?" she asked, sounding amused.

"Yes, actually. I figured you would find any way you could to hide."

"Just a personal preference," she said, watching as my hand moved up to the blanket that was just barely hiding her breasts from view.

I still hadn't gotten to see them. When she had removed her bra, her hair had been in the way. And I hadn't even thought to look when she was freaking out.

I flicked the material away.

"Fuck me." Perfect. Every inch. From her toes (the second one on her left foot turning just ever so slightly in toward the big one) to her shapely legs, to the small pinpoint of a birth mark on her ribs, to the dusty pink nipples on her breasts. Just... perfect.

My hand pressed down onto her ribs. "Ava, breathe," I told her and watched as her chest shook when she finally inhaled. My hand slid upward, the edge of my finger just barely brushing the underside of her breast. "Babe, you're perfect," I told her what I had been thinking. In my eyes, she was. "I can't wait to touch these," I admitted, my thumb stroking the soft underside of her breast. Her whole body shivered. "So sensitive," I murmured, thinking of all the ways I could exploit that, show her how wonderful that was. I forced my hand away before I crossed a line, letting it slide down her belly and making her back arch up off the mattress. Fuck. Yeah. "Okay," I said on a sigh, trying to control myself. "Why don't you roll onto your stomach sweetheart."

"Why?"

"Please," I said, the word tense. I was fucking struggling. That was new for me. I needed a few minutes to pull myself together.

She looked at me, then down my body before moving to turn. My hand grabbed her hip, sinking in for a second before I forced myself to let her go so she could roll over.

My hands moved over her soft skin as I tried to ignore the way she shifted and shivered and sucked in her breath.

Unable to help myself, my hands moved over the plump roundness of her ass, shaking my head at myself. I was never so lost before, so at the mercy of my own sex drive. Because the next second, my hand shifted to the underside of her ass, hovering over the juncture of her thighs, feeling the heat from her pussy. A pussy that I would bet my last dollar was wet.

"Are you wet for me, Ava?" Her head nodded slightly. "I can't wait to touch and taste and *feel* that." All I could comfort myself with was... soon. I would be able to run my fingers up her slick heat, stroke her clit until she was straining, push my finger inside her until she came, crying out my name. Then I could bury my face between her thighs, letting her sweetness coat my tongue as I drove her up, her legs closing around my head, her hands holding me to her. Fuck, then I could ease my throbbing cock inside her and make us both fall apart.

Soon.

My hands drifted down her thighs before I moved away. "Okay," I said, rolling onto my back and patting my chest. Don't ask me why, but I needed her there. "Come over here."

She practically flew at me, resting her head on my chest and sinking into me easily. Like we had done it a thousand times before. Like it was the most natural thing in the world.

We stayed like that for a long time, her nestled against me, my hands lazily moving up her back, through her hair, over her hip.

Until I heard her stomach growl angrily.

I chuckled and spoke before I thought it through. It came out naturally. Like it would have if we were just any two people- just a man and a woman, not patient and doctor.

"Your belly is growling. Let's go get you some food."

And with that, I crossed yet another professional line.

But there was already no going back.

After the Session

I did something I had never done before.

I dressed her.

And it was slow. And sensual. And almost as intimate as holding her.

Then she, very timidly but with steady hands, buttoned my shirt.

And I took her to a restaurant.

Like we were a normal couple on a date.

"Come on," I said, offering her my hand to help her out of the car. "Get your pretty little ass out here," I said, grinning.

"Well if you're going to put it that way," she laughed, taking my hand, moving to pull it away as soon as she was on her feet, but I held it tighter, interlocking our fingers as I led her inside.

I knew I lost her by the time I walked up to the hostess podium. She was there, walking with me, her hand in mine, but she was a million miles away. You could practically feel the wall between us. "Ava where are you?" I asked as the hostess placed the menus.

"Nowhere important," she said, shaking her head as if to clear it as she scooted into the booth and picked up her menu. She was very carefully, but also very pointedly avoiding my eye contact.

When I moved in beside her, she moved her body away. It was subtle, but it was poignant. I sighed inwardly, looking at my menu. "Doesn't matter what you order, I guarantee it will be the best Italian you've ever had."

Then she told me about her little mom and pop Italian place by her apartment, her eyes bright, her speech more open and friendly than it usually was. Inclusive. That's what it was. It was Ava, the whole package. Just the barest hint of it. Because then we were tasting the wine and she was shutting herself back away again.

"What's the matter?"

Her back immediately straightened, her entire demeanor changing. Shifting. "Nothing," she said simply.

"Don't lie, Ava," I said. My tone sounded defeated even to my own ears. "If you don't want to tell me, that's fine. But don't lie."

"Fine," she snapped. Snapped. Like she was angry. "I don't want to talk about it." Hell, she even punctuated her point with a glare in my direction. I couldn't help it. I laughed. "What?" she said, her eyes getting small.

"Kitty has claws," I said quietly as the waiter came to take our order.

The silence hung for a few minutes before I broke it. "What happened?" I asked.

"What do you mean?" she asked, her tone guarded.

"Well, each step you took from the car to the booth, you got more and more tense. And then, sitting here, staring at your menu but not actually reading it, you got positively ramrod straight. Something was going on in that head of yours."

Her tone was cold, hell, practically frigid when she spoke. "Are we on my time right now?"

"Your time?" I asked, not understanding. Not her question, but also not her tone.

"Yes, my time. Like... is this part of the whole... experience?"

The restaurant. The small talk. She wanted to know if it was part of her therapy. Shit. God damn it. "What? No," I said, shaking my head.

"Then maybe you shouldn't be trying to analyze me," she barked at me.

I felt my brow rise. "I'm not trying to analyze you, Ava. I am trying to understand why you are looking at me like I am suddenly a different person," I started. She opened her mouth to interrupt, to object, but I cut her off, "A person you hate."

"I don't hate you," she said too quickly for it to be anything other than the truth. I watched as something happened to her face. A tightness in her jaw. A gritting of her teeth. A hardening of her eyes.

"There. Right there. What are you thinking to make you look at me like that?"

"Maybe it's just my face," she brushed it off, smirking.

"No. Your face is soft and sweet and gorgeous enough to launch a thousand god damn ships." I paused, taking a breath. "Why won't you talk to me?"

"Do you do this to everyone?"

"Do what?"

"Try to browbeat them into telling you what they are thinking. Not all our thoughts are meant to be shared you know."

"I'm not..." I started to object, but she had a point. She was right. I was browbeating her. I was pushing where it wasn't my place. Which was not okay both professionally or personally. No matter how pure my motives. I exhaled a frustrated breath. "Okay. We are just going to let that go. All of it. Time for a subject change."

There was a long pause and I knew she was struggling with her social anxiety but I was honestly just in no place to be carrying the conversation so I couldn't help her out. "Do you have any siblings?"

I felt myself smile. "Ten or fifteen close ones."

I didn't tell everyone the foster care story. It wasn't a happy one. It wasn't even a neutral one. It was a giant sore spot full of nights crying in unfamiliar bedrooms surrounded by kids who I had never met who let me have my privacy to mourn over what I had lost. Because they had no comfort to offer. Because they were just giant gaping wounds like I was too.

I wasn't sure why I told her. Because she was so exposed to me? Because I wanted to even the playing field? Somehow, I didn't think that was it. I was pretty sure there was a part of me, a part of me I didn't quite understand because it didn't quite make sense, that just... wanted her to know me. Not as her doctor. Not as her surrogate. Just... as a person.

Her big brown eyes got sad when I told her, to the point of glistening for me and the little kid I used to be. Helpless. Dragged away from the only person I knew and tossed with strangers. She knew. She had tried working at child services. She couldn't stomach it. All the crying. The pain. The families torn apart. It was heartbreaking to be on the outside of it, but she knew how much worse it was to be on the inside.

Then she reached down, took my hand, and laced it with mine. When she looked up at me, I swear to Christ... her heart was in her eyes.

It was a moment I wanted to sear into my memory so I could never forget it.

But it was a moment ended to soon with the sound of our meal arriving.

"Are you going to eat or just keep pushing the lettuce around?" I asked after watching her for a minute.

And damn if she didn't stab a fork full, shove it into her mouth until it was almost too full to talk around and glowered at me. "Happy?"

I threw my head back and laughed, caught off guard yet again by another unexpected look at the real Ava.

I shook my head, reaching out and rubbing my thumb across her lip where some dressing was and brought it to my lips and licked it off. Her eyes went from teasing to downright hot. Turned on. Completely. "Having some dirty thoughts, huh?" I teased, not able to help myself.

"You wish," she said, her gaze falling from mine.

We both knew she was lying. But I was going to let it slide. "Damn straight I do."

I caught her eyeing my ziti and we ended up sharing. Well, by 'sharing' I mean she ate more of my food than I did. And she surprised me (and likely herself) by steering the conversation without needing to be prompted to. She asked me about college. Where I went. What was it like? The topics stayed safe, tame. She didn't ask about how I got into surrogacy. Not that I expected her to. That wasn't her style. She was too shy. Too worried about crossing a socially unacceptable line.

She told me more about her family who seemed like they had been overbearing as she grew up and that she had to move away from them as an adult to finally learn how to keep them at a metaphorical distance.

Too soon, the check arrived. I paid. We got into my car and we drove back to the parking garage by my office.

I got out and walked her to her car, both of us having words that we needed to say. And both of us keeping them to ourselves for our own reasons. My hand raised, wanting to stroke down her cheek. Wanting her to look at me with warmth in her eyes. But I had already crossed too many lines. My hand dropped numbly by my side. "Monday. Seven," I said, then got in my car. I waited for her to get into hers and get it started, then pulled away.

What the fuck had I gotten myself into?

I parked in front of my apartment building, nodding at the concierge as I made my way to the elevator, riding in it in a surly kind of silence. I was mad at both myself and what seemed to be an impossible situation.

The doors dinged as they opened and I moved out only to stop short.

"Chase, man," a man's voice reached me, making my head snap to search for it. Then there he was. Eddie. A year older than me. Sitting beside my apartment door like he had been there a while, a silver flask halfway to his mouth as if he wasn't fucked up enough to begin with.

"Eddie," I said, feeling resignation replace everything else inside. "What are you doing here?"

"Can't a man come see his foster brother?" he slurred, pushing himself up off the ground.

I moved to help him up, wincing when he wavered on his feet. Eddie was one of the ten or fifteen that I told Ava I kept close. Why... I wasn't sure. Maybe because of the one time when I was eight and trying to walk home from school when two kids two grades older than me started pushing me around. Eddie came out from nowhere, only a year older but street smart and scrappy, and let out a slew of curses and threats that I hardly even understood, but the kids threw up their hands and walked away. They never messed with me again.

Or maybe it was the time when we had both reconnected in a group home when I was sixteen and he came in bloodied and bruised from getting caught trying to pick someone's pocket... but he came in smiling and he treated me to pizza.

Maybe it was just because he was so damaged. So broken from a hard life that gave him nothing but memories he wanted to drown in bottles or in needles. Guilt because I had gotten out, made a good life for myself while my savior from when I was eight and helpless had turned out to be someone who so completely needed saving himself.

"Sure, man," I said, letting him into my apartment, but took his flask. It was something that was so common between us that he didn't even bother to fight it anymore. He knew he wouldn't win, not if he wanted a place to crash. "Have you eaten?"

"Not hungry," he said, shrugging out of his jacket. It took him three tries to get it on the hook by the door.

Eddie worked construction. Mostly it paid well enough. It didn't require education. The foreman didn't have much to say when he showed up hungover every morning. He was, therefore, built like a construction worker- tall, broad, strong. Shaggy blonde hair and tan with almost unsettling hazel eyes.

"How have you been?" I asked, shrugging out of my jacket and watching him walk over to my windows and look out.

"Same ole'," he said, shrugging.

"You need a place to stay for a few days?"

"Yeah. Just 'till Monday or Tuesday. I have a place lined up." He paused, moving toward the stereo and clicking through the playlists. "Want to go to a gig on Saturday?" he asked, meaning there was one of his local bands playing. Music, the only thing that kept him halfway sane. He was the one who created all the play lists on my stereo at the office.

"I have to go to the group home," I reminded him, like I always had to remind him. He winced at the mention of that place. Like he always did. Like I always used to. Until I got my degree and decided to use it to turn an awful memory into one I could live with- working there on Saturdays offering up my time for any of the kids who wanted someone to talk to. Someone who had been where they were. "But if it's after six, sure."

"Knew I could count on you, brother," he said, lowering himself onto the couch. Before the first song could come to an end, he was asleep.

I sighed, grabbing the alcohol off the sidebar and locking it up. He would respect my wishes when I was around to see him. But all bets were off if he found himself alone with a bottle. And I wanted a morning with him where he wasn't drunk off his ass.

When he was clean, he was one of the best guys around. Unfortunately, no matter how many treatment programs I got him into, Eddie was never clean for more than two weeks at a time after he got out.

I gave him a blanket and went to my room, lying down and trying to think of anything other than Ava perfect freaking Davis.

Obviously, I failed.

Third Session

I still had Eddie on my couch.

And as much as it bothered me to see him stumble around drunk or high, I liked having him around. I guess that made me an enabler. His stay would end like all previous ones had- with me trying to convince him to go back into detox and rehab, reminding him he had my support, often going with him on the group therapy days.

But I owed it to him.

He saved me and I was never going to stop trying to save him.

Besides, it was nice to not go home to an empty apartment every night. Hell, the guy even cooked when he was clear-headed enough to remember how to use the stove.

So he was on my mind as I shuffled though paperwork I had my receptionist print out for various clinics for him. After all the years, he had cornered the market on most of the close ones and I was having to branch out. That was where my head was when the door open, slammed, and I heard someone fall back against it.

My head snapped up to find Ava collapsed against the door, dressed in black leggings and a sand-colored sweater that was so large it completely swallowed her body up.

But that wasn't what got me. What got me was she was completely and utterly wrecked. Anxious. Pale. She had huge bags under her eyes from sleeplessness.

"Ava..."

"Please please," she started, holding up a hand to silence me. "Please just tell me what this session is."

Fuck.

I felt my shoulders fall as I tilted my head. "Oh, baby," I said, already crossing the floor toward her, pulling her away from the door and wrapping my arms around her. Unable to stop myself, I kissed the top of her hair. "Next time you're this anxious about needing to know something, you call me. I don't want you stressing over something I can easily fix. Actually," I said, reaching for her hand and prying her phone from between her fingers, "I will give you my cell so that, no matter what time it is, you can call me and I can talk you down. Okay?"

"Okay," she said, her voice hollow. "You still haven't answered me."

"I know," I said, half untangling myself from her body, wrapping my arm around her waist and guiding her through my office and into the bedroom. She refused drinks and put on another safe playlist. "Babe, how long has it been since you've slept?"

There was a weird shaky laugh before, "For how long?"

I felt my eyes rolling. "For more than an hour at a time."

"Wednesday."

Jesus Christ.

"Next time, you call me," I told her, putting her phone down on the sidebar, taking her hand, and leading her over to the bed. I kicked out of my shoes and took off my jacket before moving into the bed. There was a moment of hesitation before she was out of her shoes and beside me. Not touching, just both of us lying there side by side.

I wasn't going to reach for her, to possibly freak her out more than she already was. So I waited.

In the end, I didn't even have to wait long. Her body shifted, curling into my side. Then, to my complete and utter shock, she unbuttoned my shirt. Quickly. Efficiently. With sure fingers. Then she moved the sides apart and laid her head down on my chest. My arm went around her, squeezing her a bit too hard, like I wanted to anchor her to me for what I was about to say.

"Tonight's session is about masturbation."

She stiffened and choked out, "What about it?"

"Everything about it. We will talk about it. Then we will undress. And then we will do it."

"Wait. What?" she asked, her voice a strange high-pitched squeak. Every cell in her body on edge.

"Ava, calm down. I know it's an uncomfortable topic for a lot of people. Actually, this might be one of the hardest lessons. It's understandable that you feel awkward or embarrassed. That's totally normal."

Most people, average well adjusted people didn't masturbate in front of their partners. It was somehow an ingrained embarrassment. For both sexes.

"Do you?" she asked.

"No baby," I answered carefully. While there may have been a time when that was the case, it was long gone. Both personally and professionally. "But listen, there is nothing at all to feel embarrassed about. A woman making herself feel good is amazing. *You* making yourself feel good? That is going to be fucking beautiful. And I can't wait to see it." I paused, letting my mind wander for the barest of moments. "Are you more uncomfortable with watching me masturbate or having me watch you?" I asked, already pretty sure of the answer.

"You watching me," she admitted, the sound muffled and I looked down to see she had her face buried in her hands.

"Okay. Then I will start first." I pressed her back onto the mattress and stood beside the bed, slipping out of my shirt and moving to the zipper of my pants. "Don't be shy in front of me baby," I said, wanting her to get up and start stripping as well. She didn't fight. She didn't even stall. She simply sat up, pushed down her leggings, and pulled off her sweater, leaving her sitting there in simple black panties and a black bra. "And the rest?" I asked, hearing my voice get husky. She was somehow sexier in in plain cotton panties than most women were in three hundred dollar lingerie. She reached behind her back for the clasp of her bra and quickly discarded it away, then laid back to shimmy out of her panties. "Beautiful," I said, just as naked as her as I climbed into the bed. "Come here," I said as I lay back.

Then she simply... flew at me. Like the only thing that could make her feel better was being as close to me as possible. Fuck if that didn't feel good. It shouldn't have, because she was just a client. But it did. I stifled the suspicion that that was because I wanted her to be more than that.

To distract myself, my hand slid confidently down my body, grabbing my cock and starting to stroke. "Are you watching?" I asked, though her head had already shifted and I knew she was.

"Yes," she said almost too quietly to be heard.

"I want to watch you baby," I said, letting my arm release her. "Please."

She was turned on. There was no mistaking it. It was in her shallow, quick breathing. It was in the flush on her cheeks and chest. It was in the way her legs kept shifting against the raging desire between them.

She took a deep breath and her hand started trailing down her body. Her legs parted just wide enough for her hand to slip in and her fingers slipped between them, stroking up her pussy and making a surprised whimper escape her lips.

I almost fucking came right then and there.

It was the hottest thing I had ever witnessed before.

"Don't stop, Ava," I said and her eyes moved to find mine. "Please don't stop." Her hand shifted upward on her pussy, finding her clit, and circling it. "There you go. Just like I said... fucking beautiful."

And it was.

Her eyes fell from mine and moved down my body, watching as I stroked my cock as she worked her fingers over herself.

Not a minute later, I lost her. Her body got stiff. Her hand went lax between her thighs. She was lost somewhere inside.

My hand dropped my cock. "Ava," I said and her eyes rose to me. "There you are," I said, giving her a small smile before my lips crushed down on hers. Hard. Passionate. Full of all the longing I was feeling in that moment. I wanted to show it to her. I wanted her to take it on as her own. It wasn't long before her body came alive again, a low whimpering from her lips, a writhing. Then a jolt through her whole body. My touch. My touch was what got her out of her head. *Fuck me.*

"Touch yourself, baby. Think of me doing it."

And, fuck, how I wanted to be the one doing it.

But it had to be her. This time it had to be her.

Her fingers started moving across her clit again, her lips falling slightly apart, her back arching off of the bed.

I stroked my cock again, alternating between watching her face as it twisted in desire and watching her hand between her legs.

She was getting close.

Then she was gone again. This time she was not just distant, but completely pale with some memory. I found myself wishing I could wipe those from her psyche, give her a fresh start. Nothing should have been able to stop her from enjoying her own touch. Nothing. But something was.

My hand moved from her shoulder and, while I knew I shouldn't, I put my hand down on top her hers between her legs.

She needed it. She needed me. It was the only thing that was going to pull her back.

"Be here. With me," I said, my fingers crooking inward and pressing hers harder against her clit and she gasped. "Yeah, like that. Keep your eyes on me."

So she did. Her eyes held mine as her fingers went to work between her thighs. My hand stayed there, but didn't assist. I just kept her grounded to me as she drove herself up. Moaning. Back arching. Legs moving across the mattress. Hips rising to meet her strokes.

Fuck.

We were both close.

"So sexy," I said, feeling my body get tense as my orgasm threatened.

Her head tilted up and my lips pressed into hers, wanting the intimacy, wanting to share the moment.

Then she pulled suddenly back. Her breath caught. Her eyes got wide.

"That's it. Come for me, baby."

Then she did.

And it was *hard*.

Her body went taut. A loud cry escaped her lips as she shook through her orgasm, her hand slamming down on my chest.

Fucking beautiful.

Nothing came close.

Spent, she shifted closer, curling into me. Her hand pulled away and I moved mine. Not away. Just nestled between her closed thighs, feeling her heat and wetness there and it was my undoing.

I came hard, my body jerking, my hand digging into her inner thigh. "Fuck, Ava," I growled, stroking a few more times until I was completely spent.

Then she did the sweetest fucking thing. She snuggled into my neck and planted a kiss at the bottom of my throat as I tried to slow my breathing.

I tilted my head down, kissing her forehead. "Let me up, babe," I said, needing to go clean up. It was clearly not a plan she was all that happy about as she made a grumbling noise and rolled off of me, making me chuckle as I got up and walked toward the bathroom.

I washed up quickly but in the time it took me to get back to her, she was snuggled deep into the blankets, eyes at half-mast, bone deep tired from all the sleeplessness and likely aggravated by her orgasm. I smiled down at her as I slipped underneath the covers. I pulled her to my chest. "It's okay. Get some sleep," I told her, my other arm wrapping her tight. "I'm right here."

And she was right there.

And I had a sneaking feeling that was where I would always want her to be.

Fuck, fuck me.

After the Session

I woke up alone.

Which normally wasn't a big deal.

But I woke up alone in a bed in my office when I had fallen asleep with a very soft, very contented Ava wrapped up with me. An Ava who had proven herself a practiced worrywart, capable of turning a situation that had gone well, that had made her (and by extension, me) happy, and twist it into something dark.

Fuck.

I never got dressed that fast in my life, still buttoning my shirt as I looked through the room, my office, then reception for some kind of note explaining what happened. I grabbed my keys and phone and made my way to the door. Which was locked. That made no damn sense whatsoever.

I went out, scrolling through my contacts until I found her entry, and hit send.

"This is Ava. Please leave a message."

Was she ignoring my calls? Or was she genuinely out of reach?

I called again. And again. And again.

If it was any other woman, I'd have been fucking embarrassed to let so many calls go unanswered. But she wasn't any other woman. She was shy, sweet, tortured little Ava and I was worried.

On a curse, I slammed my car door and turned back toward my office, still trying to reach her.

It was crossing a line. It was crossing *all kinds* of lines. But I looked up her address. Then I drove my ass to her apartment. I banged on her door loud enough to wake all of her neighbors.

I heard the locks slide and the door swung open. Then there she was. In pajamas. With sleep-hooded eyes. *Thank fuck.*

"Chase?" she asked, her light brows drawing together like she wasn't sure if she was seeing what she was seeing.

"Jesus Christ, woman," I growled to myself, running a anxious hand through my hair.

"Chase, what are you doing here?"

"You scared the fuck out of me," I admitted.

"What?"

"I woke up alone. I woke up alone and there was no note or anything. And my front door was somehow locked."

She skipped over everything else I said and focused on the damn door topic. "I fiddled with it with one of my keys until it finally clicked."

"I called your phone... I don't know... twenty-five times."

"Oh," she said, her mouth pouting slightly as she looked to the side of the door where, I assumed, her phone must have been. "I didn't have it with me," she said. Then, taking a deep breath as if she needed to muster her courage, she asked, "Chase, why are you here?"

"I got up. You were gone. No note. You didn't answer your cell..."

"You were... worried about me?" she interrupted in a tone that suggested it was the most asinine idea she had ever heard.

"Hell fucking yeah I was worried about you," I said, shaking my head. "What did I say about walking around at night? Not just at night. It must have been like... two in the morning. That was taking an unnecessary risk. You should have woken me up so I could walk you."

"Chase I have been walking myself around this city alone, even at night, for years."

"Taking stupid chances," I pressed. How could she not see how defenseless she truly was? If someone ever came out of an alley... "Looking like you do, you should have someone on you all the time."

"It's... sweet of you to worry about me and I'm sorry I didn't leave a note or answer my phone. I just... didn't want to wake you."

"I can always get more sleep. I can't get another you."

Fuck.

That slipped out.

I hadn't meant to say that out loud.

Damn it.

"What?" she asked, her eyes going a bit wide at my admission that was way too close to admitting the whole truth about how I felt.

"Nothing," I said, hoping for casual as I shrugged and looked away from her.

"What the hell is going on?" a male voice joined us, making Ava start and my face to snap around, a swirling in my stomach akin to jealousy starting. Until I saw Jake, the asshole roommate, walking out of his room with pants he had obviously hastily thrown on. "Ava who the hell is at the door at this... oh," he stopped, eyeing me. He looked sheepish. As he should. "Dr. Hudson," he said, inclining his head.

"Get back in here and finish fucking m..." yet another voice joined. This time female. I looked past Jake to where a black-haired girl came running out of Jake's room wearing nothing but a god damn diamond pendant necklace. "Oh, well, *hello*," she purred at me, her eyes giving me a slow once-over.

Normally, she would have been my type. Secure. Sexually confident. Unafraid of her own desires.

But, in that moment, she simply paled into the background.

She had nothing on the sleepy-eyed, but suddenly quite horrified, shy, insecure Ava standing a few feet from me.

"Hi," I clipped to her, looking back at Ava with a raised brow, willing her to stand her ground. Trying to get her to *do something* about a situation that was obviously making her uncomfortable.

"Um, Jake?" she started, her voice a little soft, but I knew she was trying.

"Yeah?" he asked, completely oblivious to the awkwardness of the situation.

"I'm pretty sure we agreed to a *no naked in the main area of the house* rule."

Jake looked between us and shrugged, "Yeah sure," he said and addressed his fuck buddy. "Get back in that room and get yourself started," he instructed and Ava's face went red.

I fought the smile I felt tugging at my lips. She was embarrassed. It wasn't because of Jake's naked girl. It wasn't even because of Jake's mention that she get herself started. It was because she was thinking about us masturbating together.

"You sure you guys are alright out here?" Jake asked, addressing Ava and I wondered if he had always been halfway decent about taking care of her or if it was because I scolded him at the bar a few days before.

"Yeah, Jake. Fine," she said, addressing her own feet.

"Alright," he said, nodding at me. He bent low into Ava's ear and whispered something that made her cheeks blaze all the more.

71

"This is an interesting place you live in," I said, holding in a chuckle, partly because that was just a fucking ridiculous interaction and partly because she was so damn embarrassed about it. "Ava," I said, my tone more serious. But she just kept looking down at her feet. I let my eyes drop, taking in her bright neon green toenail polish with a smile before reaching my hand out to lift her face to mine. "What's going on in that little head of yours?" I wondered out loud. "You're blushing."

"I think it's polite to *not* say that to someone who is, in fact, blushing," she chastened gently.

"Are you blushing because of that comment your roommate made?" I asked, already knowing my answer.

"What comment?" she asked, feigning ignorance.

"The one where he told her to get started without him. Ah, I thought so," I smiled, sliding my thumb over the apples of her cheeks as they got redder. "Are you embarrassed that I saw you touch yourself tonight?"

"Shh," she urged, her head going over her shoulder to check and make sure Jake wasn't lingering around.

I laughed. "They sound like they're going to break through the wall. They can't hear us."

She turned back to me, looking uncomfortable as she cleared her throat. "But, yeah, sorry again for making you worry..."

"It's alright," I said, trying to force myself to distance myself from her. My hand dropped. "I'm gonna go." I *had* to go before I pushed into her apartment and fucked everything up. "Keep your phone by you. It's a safety thing," I said. "And lock your door." I paused in my orders, watching as a fully amused smile overtook her features. It was truly the first of its kind I had gotten to see and it sent a stab through my chest. "What?" I asked, wanting to know what she was thinking.

"You're bossy," she said, almost giggling.

I felt myself laugh and snort at the same time, shaking my head. She had no idea. "Phone and lock, okay?"

"Okay," she agreed and she was fighting a smile.

72

I needed to *fucking go*.

"Tomorrow night. Seven."

I didn't even wait for a response, just turned on my heel and got out of there as fast as I could without it looking like I was running. But I was fucking running.

I drove home trying to convince myself to sever ties with her. It was the right thing to do. Truly, the only thing to do. On a professional level. That was supposed to be all that mattered to me. I worked my ass off to get my career. I had never done anything that could ever even remotely threaten it before.

But I was all kinds of line crossing with Ava.

I just couldn't fucking shake the idea that maybe she was worth the risk.

"You're late," Eddie said, making a surprised laugh escape my lips. He sounded like an angry wife when her husband didn't call to tell her he was going to miss dinner. "Get laid?" he asked, giving me one of his lopsided smiles and I realized his eyes weren't bleary from booze or dilated from drugs.

"Work," I clarified. It was mostly true.

Eddie nodded his head, moving toward the kitchen and getting a glass of water. *Water*. "Surrogate work, right?" he asked, drinking.

"Yeah," I nodded, pulling off my tie.

"Subs," Eddie said, watching me.

"What? I asked, slipping out of my jacket too.

"I'm on subs. That's why I'm not fucked up."

"You went to the clinic?" I asked, so surprised I froze mid stride.

That wasn't like him. He never acted without my spurring him into it. At least not when it came to recovery. There was never a trip to a session that I didn't drive him to. Or a clinic visit to get suboxone. Or a trip to the pharmacy to make sure he didn't use the maintenance drugs to get high.

Eddie shrugged, looking away from me. "Thought maybe it was time for you to stop having to take care of me."

"Eddie, man..."

He shook his head, silencing me. "Been leanin' on you too long. Need to get on my own feet."

He was right. He did.

But still.

"If you need anything though..."

"I know," he said, nodding at me. "Now go get some sleep. It's fucking late."

It was, so I moved into my bedroom and undressed. I lay down in bed. But sleep wouldn't come.

Before I even knew what I was doing, I picked up my phone and dialed.

"Hello?" Ava's hesitant voice met my ear.

"Take your clothes off."

"What?" she asked, sounding suddenly alert.

"Take your clothes off, baby," I said, my tone gentler. She wasn't ready for the demanding side of me. She probably never would be. Not in the course of ten sessions anyway.

"Why?"

I chuckled softly, shaking my head in the dark of my room. "How about you don't fight me on everything?"

"Why could you possibly want to..."

"We are going to masturbate together again," I told her, my cock already throbbing in need.

"Oh," came her surprised reply followed by a long enough silence that I knew she was starting to freak out.

"I can hear those gears turning. Just take off your clothes and lay back down, okay?"

"Is this... part of the... program?"

No fucking way.

And I should have been hanging up.

I should never have called in the first place.

"Yeah, baby," I lied instead, closing my eyes against the lead feeling settling in my stomach at doing so.

I could hear rustling for a minute and an image of her stripping out of her clothes flashed in front of my eyes. "Are you naked?"

"Yes."

"So am I."

"Chase..." her shy voice reached my ear.

"Run your hand down your body," I told her, cutting her off and cutting through her insecurity. My hand moved as I imagined hers did as well.

"Okay."

"Are you wet baby?" I asked, grabbing my cock.

A short pause before, "Yes." Her voice was airy. Turned on. Fuck me.

"Mmm. Touch yourself. And I am going to touch myself. Just... relax. Let me hear you."

The silence stretched on for a long minute before her breath became faster, a hitching evident on each inhale and the sound sent a surge of desire right to my cock.

"Does that feel good?" I needed to hear her. Not just her breathing. *Her.* I needed to hear *her.* I had expected a timid 'yes'. What I got was way better. What I got was a unexpected moan. "Fuck baby. You sound so sweet when you moan." After that, the moans and whimpers came fast and frantic and I knew she was close. I was too.

"Chase?" her voice reached to me.

"Let me hear you come, Ava."

Then, as if she had been waiting for the command all along, she did. With a loud half-gasp, half-cry that pushed me over the edge along with her. "Fuck," I growled as I came hard.

I took a few deep breaths, standing to get cleaned up. On the other end of the phone, I could hear her breathing slow to normal.

"Ava?"

"I'm here," she said, sounding both sleepy and contented at once. I ignored the warmth I felt in my chest, pushing that shit away to be dealt with at another time. Or never. Never worked for me too.

A million things flashed in my head to say.

Not one of them appropriate.

In the end, though, I sighed to myself.

"Tomorrow at seven."

Then I hung up, knowing sleep was never going to come.

Fourth Session

"You're out?" I asked, watching Eddie stuff his clothes back into his bag.

"Place is ready," he said, zipping his bag and moving into the kitchen. "Thanks for letting me crash."

"Anytime," I said, watching him collect his wallet and keys.

The leaving was the worst. Even when he was drunk or high off his ass when he was staying with me, there was a sort of comfort in knowing I was around to keep an eye on him. I was there to make sure he didn't get alcohol poisoning or OD on whatever the drug of the week was. Him heading back out always had a swirling pitfall feeling in my stomach. Knowing he was alone. No one would be around to look for the signs of shit going south.

But he was a grown ass man and I couldn't stop him.

So he was leaving.

And I would just have to deal.

"Do you want me to go to any of your appointments with you?" I asked, shrugging into my suit jacket.

"Chase," he said, his tone serious enough to make me look up. "You've taken care of me for long enough. I got this."

Then he turned and was out the door.

I got this.

That was what he told me the day before he OD'd the first time when he was eighteen and out on his own and I was still stuck at the group home.

I was praying I wasn't going to get that call again as I made my way to the office.

I was bone-deep tired after a night of no sleep. And I still had ten hours before my appointment with Ava.

"Hey babe," I said, wincing at myself when she walked in wearing jeans and a simple long-sleeve purple tee. I had to stop calling her pet names. Had to. "You look nice." Jesus fuck. What was wrong with me?

Something came across her face at my words then that cut through my internal chastisement. It was something that didn't fit on her face right. There was a tension in her jaw that made her lips turn down ever so slightly and lowering of her brows that spoke of something I couldn't quite place. Anger? Resentment? Coldness? Something akin to those emotions. Something that didn't belong to Ava.

"What's with the look?"

"Nothing," she said practically before I stopped speaking, shaking her head and the look drained from her face.

"Want a drink?" I asked, needing one myself.

"Sure," she shrugged, following me through to the bedroom and going to the stereo to choose a playlist.

I mixed drinks as a blues playlist came on. It wasn't just any blues playlist. It was a sad one. It was labeled specifically for that purpose. I *knew* something was up.

"Want to talk about it?" I asked, handing her a martini.

"Talk about what?"

"Whatever is making you tense and play sad music."

"I *knew* the music thing was some kind of test," she accused, lowering her eyes at me in mock anger. "Sneaky."

I felt my lips quirk up and shrugged. It was sneaky. It was also a really good way to figure out someone like Ava-someone who would rather sell her kidneys on the black market than tell you what she was really feeling. "It's a good way to get an idea what kind of mental state a pat..." I couldn't even get the word out. She wasn't a fucking patient. "*Someone* is in," I said instead.

The look came back. Stronger. It was a quick flash that pushed away something else that almost looked like pain from her eyes. "Clever," she said, draining her drink and putting it aside. "I'm assuming this is a clothes-off session again," she said, her voice off, almost a little hollow.

"Yes," I said, nodding.

"Okay," she said and her hands went immediately to her jeans, unfastening them and pushing them down. She was out of them before I could even draw a breath. Her hands went to the hem of her shirt. She took it off in one quick jerk, leaving her there in just her bra and panties, every ounce of her seeming to spark with tension. But not anxiety. Not nerves. Something else. But damn if I could figure out what it was.

"Ava... what's going on?"

"What do you mean?" she asked, hands dropping from the clasp of her bra. "This is what I am supposed to be doing, right?"

I swallowed past the irritation I felt building. "Maybe if you communicated with me instead of assuming things, you would already know the answer to that," I said, putting my drink down. "Talk to me."

"It's nothing. Jake said something that put me in a bad mood," she said but it rang only half true to my ears.

"Come here," I said, holding open my arms. She moved into my arms and I wrapped them around her, feeling her hands slip up my back and dig into the material of my jacket. "Tonight I wanted to undress you," I admitted, briefly letting the longing slip into my words. It was my turn. Finally. I could touch her. Not just her back or her hair. We were at the point where I could... *touch her.* And I wanted to start that by slowly lifting her shirt, then getting to my knees to help her out of her pants. I wanted to look up at her with my face level with her heat and see her eyes lit with desire.

"Sorry," she said, sounding like she genuinely meant it, like she was sad she missed out on that opportunity too.

"It's okay. I still have some things to remove," I said, my hands sliding up her soft back to rest over the clasps of her bra.

"Am I going to undress you?" she asked, her words muffled against my chest.

"Yeah, baby."

Then I felt myself stiffen because her hands went up between our bodies, the closeness making her palms press hard against my stomach as she slowly started unfastening the buttons of my shirt. I couldn't tell you if I was more pleased by her sudden boldness or more worried about it. It just simply wasn't like her.

Her hands reached the top button and they slipped underneath the material, gathering it and my jacket and pushing them back to move them off my body. I released her just long enough to let that happen, then rested one hand on her hip, the other going to the side of her neck, trying to get her to face me. "Ava..."

She shook her head at me and her hands went for my belt. Her hands slipped inside the waistband of my slacks as she undid the button. I was hard. And I mean... *hard.* That was all it took. She pushed my pants down and I slipped off my socks and shoes before stepping out of the legs. Before I could even finish, her hands went to my boxer briefs, not even pausing before pushing them down, leaving me completely naked before her.

Her gaze was fixated down, looking at my cock and a weird noise got caught in her throat. "Ava," I said, my tone firm, and her eyes rose to mine. "While I'm glad you're taking the lead, babe," I said, my hand moving from her neck to her cheek, "I want to make sure it's for the right reasons."

Her lips pursed like she was thinking. "Are there... *wrong* reasons to undress you?" she asked, then her hands moved to stroke over my abs and I couldn't fucking think of a good enough response to that question.

"Fine. I'll let it go for now. But I will get to the bottom of it eventually," I vowed. "Go get on the bed."

Christ. Not only did I need to knock it off with the pet names, I needed to stop being so bossy with her.

She simply moved away from me and went to lie down.

I climbed in with her, moving to sit on me heels beside her, reaching behind her back and unclasping her bra. I worked the straps down her arms, leaving the cups to keep her hidden until her arms were free, then pulling the material away.

Fuck me.

It felt like I had been waiting so long for that moment.

That moment when my hand reached out and brushed over one of her perfect breasts, feeling a shiver move through her whole body at the contact. My eyes lifted to her face as my hand brushed across her chest again, watching as her lips parted, feeling her back arch off the mattress, pressing her breast further into my hand.

Christ. She was going to be my fucking undoing

My fingers moved to her nipple, rolling it between my fingers and she sucked in a shaky breath. "You okay?"

"Yeah," she said, her tone breathless, needy.

"Thank god," I said, moving to her other breast, rolling that nipple to a hardened point. "You have no idea how hard it has been not to touch you. This is what we are doing this session," I said, looking down at my hands. "I am going to touch you here," I said, squeezing her breast slightly as my other hand moved a slow line down her belly until it rested over the juncture of her closed thighs, "and here." I paused, letting that sink in, seeing a bit of anxiety bubble up. "Look at me, Ava," I said, waiting for her eyes to find my face. "I am going to touch you. And you are going to touch me." I gave her another second. "Do you think it would be better for me to touch you first or..."

"Me touch you," she blurted out, cutting me off.

"You're sure?" I asked.

"Yes," she said, sounding mostly confident in her decision.

"Okay," I said, pulling my hands from her and she made an objection sound in her throat as I moved to sit upright against the headboard. "Come here," I said, holding out an arm and she slid into my body.

She was tense. Even with me holding her. Her body was taut. Her breathing shallow. I reached for her hand, interlocking our fingers, and squeezed. "You nervous?"

"A little." More like a lot. But I wasn't going to push it.

"A little isn't bad, right?" I asked instead, running my free hand up and down her arm. "Give me a number."

"Four... ish," she decided, taking a slow, deep breath, her nose close to my chest as if she was trying to breathe me in.

"I can work with fourish. How about the idea of me touching you?"

"Seven?"

"I can work with that too," I said, untangling my fingers from hers and pressing her palm against my chest, my hand over hers. "But let's not think about that yet, alright?"

"Alright."

I slid her hand down my chest, my stomach, the muscles twitching under the contact, down my pelvic bone. My cock was so hard it was painful as her palm moved down my happy trail. But then she tensed. Her hand curled into my skin like she could hold on. I smiled down at the top of her head, pulling her hand up toward my face and kissing it before pushing it down the same path. That time much more quickly. Until I helped her wrap her hand around my cock. Her hand instinctively tightened and I felt my cock twitch as I groaned. "That's it. Touch me, baby," I encouraged, my hand dropping from hers.

Then she did. She was a little hesitant at first. Her hand stroked upward, her thumb circling over the head and I groaned again, my body going stiff as her hand got more sure with each stroke. Up and down. Then up and down with a twisting motion, making my hand dig into her arm as the pressure built.

"That feels good, baby," I told her, wanting her to know she was doing well, wanting her to feel good about herself as she stroked me toward fucking oblivion. My hand moved over hers for a second, squeezing her hand so it grabbed me harder. "Just a little harder," I told her, letting my hand fall. Her hand gripped me as she continued her stroking. "Yeah, just like that," I said, tilting my head up to the ceiling, eyes closed, letting the sensation of her jerking me off overwhelm my body. I wanted to get completely fucking lost in it.

Her head tilted up and I tilted mine down to look at her. She was watching my face with an avid sort of fascination. "Fuck," I growled, feeling her finger stroke over the head again, knowing I was close. "I'm gonna come," I told her, my hand grabbing her shoulder, the other crushing into the wrist of the hand driving me toward the edge. "Fuck... *Ava*..." I growled as my orgasm coursed through me, coming hard and fast, making my body jerk in the sensation.

Spent, my body went lax and I looked to find Ava watching me still. I leaned down, pressing a kiss into her forehead and she smiled up at me. *Huge*. Happy. Proud of herself. And, fuck, I was proud of her too. So I smiled back.

"I made you feel good," she said, her tone shy.

"Yeah you did," I said, nodding, then leaned forward and took her lips. I pressed into them, letting my tongue slip in and toy with hers until that was all there was in the world. Us.

Connected. Until I started to wonder if that was all I ever wanted there to be.

On that thought, I tore my mouth from hers. "I'll be right back," I said, sliding away from her and moving toward the bathroom to clean up. I needed to get some semblance of control back. I soaped up a washcloth and went out to clean my come off her hand before discarding the washcloth and climbing back into bed with her again.

"Are the nerves better?"

"A little," she admitted, lying on her side to face me.

"Good," I said, brushing the hair off her neck and lowering my mouth there. A sigh escaped her lips at the contact. "Because I really want to make you feel good. I want to watch you as I make you come. And just when you start to come down, I am going to drive you back up and make it happen again. Until your body can't take anymore." Her eyes went wide. But not with fear or anxiety. No... with heat. "Does that sound good?"

"Yes," she sighed.

"Good," I said, pushing a hand on her shoulder until she was lying flat on her back and my hand went to her breast, toying with one and then the other until her body was writhing under my touch, until she was crushing her thighs together to ease the ache.

My hand went to the center of her chest, brushing down her belly, down one thigh, then up the other. My hand rested at the closure of her thighs, waiting. "Let me in, baby." Her legs spread open for me and I wasted no time. I had been wanting to touch her from the second I laid eyes on her in my office. I wanted to spread her and feel her heat, to plunge my fingers into it, then my tongue, my cock.

My finger traced up her pussy, finding it drenched. "You're so wet for me," I told her, fingers teasing her delicate folds but avoiding her clit. "Is this okay?" I asked, praying like fuck she didn't say no.

But what I got was a pained whimper of, "Yes."

That was what I needed to hear.

My hand moved up, circling over her clit and her entire body jolted hard at the contact. "Fuck," I growled, moving across it in slow circles, watching her arch off the bed, her eyes closed. "Ava, look at me." Then she did and I stroked her no more than two more times before her eyes went wide, her mouth parted, and her orgasm started. "Ah," she cried out hard, loud, her hands slamming into my shoulders as her body shook through her climax.

"God, you're so fucking beautiful when you come," I said, leaning across her to claim her lips. And she kissed me back. Greedily. I pulled away and waited for her eyes to open again, sliding my finger away from her clit and almost chuckling when she grumbled. "Don't worry, you're going to come again," I told her, sliding my finger down to the entrance to her pussy and pressing against it. When she didn't tense, I slid my finger into her wet, tight depths, almost groaning myself at the sensation. "You with me?" I asked once my finger was fully inside her.

"Always," she said, shocking the shit out of me, the words landing with a weighted feeling in my chest that I had to fight to not focus on as I turned my finger inside her, crooking, and stroking over her g-spot.

"Oh my god," she cried, her fingers digging into my back.

I felt my lips quirk up. "Does that feel good?"

"Yes," she moaned, her hips moving against my hand, trying to get some relief.

Unable to help myself, I started finger fucking her. Hard. Fast. The way I wanted to be able to actually fuck her, feeling her pussy tighten around my cock, feeling her nails scraping across my shoulders, her legs pulling me tightly against her, hearing her begging for release in my ear.

Her moans got faster, higher-pitched. She was close.

I stopped thrusting. I stroked over her g-spot as my thumb found her clit at the same time. And she just... shattered.

"Chase," she cried, crushing her body to mine, holding onto me.

"It's okay. I'm right here. Come baby."

She came hard and long, her pussy spasming around my finger for ages before she started to come down, her body trembling slightly. I wiggled my finger again, seeing if she could take any more. But she shook her head.

"No?" I asked.

"I can't," she said, flinging herself into me, burying her face in my chest. My hand slid away from her pussy, moving to stroke across her hips, her back, trying to bring her back down fully. "Talk to me," I said, my voice low and coaxing. But then I felt the tears sliding onto my skin. I heard the hitch in her breath as she tried to cry silently. "Babe? Ava..." I said, shifting, grabbing her face and forcing it up to mine. "Oh, sweetheart," I said, my chest constricting as my fingers brushed the tears away. "Are these good tears or bad tears?" I asked and she turned her face into my hand, kissing my palm. Thank god. "Good tears," I concluded, feeling the tightness lessen. I leaned down, kissing her tear-stained cheeks, kissing her eyelids, then finally taking her lips.

A while later, both of us sated, nearly sleepy, I shook my head at the room at large. "That was fucking amazing," I said, smiling. Because, well, it was. "I'm serious. You did really well tonight."

Apparently, that was not the right thing to say. Why? I had no fucking idea. But the look was back in her eyes, her jaw tight. And while she forced a smile, I knew it was just for show. "Where are you going?" I asked, sitting up, trying to reach for her as she all but flew away from me and got off the bed.

She didn't answer because she wasn't with me anymore. She was somewhere trapped inside as she dragged her clothes on faster than I had ever seen someone do before. Like she needed the barrier. Like she needed to get away from me as fast as possible.

I had no reason, no good, solid, professional reason to try to make her stay.

All I had were weak, flimsy, personal fucking reasons that I had no business having, let alone sharing with her.

I moved off to the side of the bed, putting my feet on the floor, resting my elbows on my legs, and holding my head in my hands.

How the fuck did I let this happen?

"Hey," she broke in, sounding almost concerned. "Are you okay?"

I took a breath, not looking at her. "Yup," I lied. "So ya' leaving me?" I asked.

"It's... late. I have work in the morning."

"Okay. Thursday. Seven-thirty." Hell, my words sounded dead even to my own ears.

"Umm," she started and I could feel her looking at me. But I couldn't look back. If I looked back, I was going to lose control and fuck the whole thing up. Hell, fuck everything in my life up. She shifted her feet. "Okay," she said in a tone that almost matched mine. Numb. Hollow. "I'll... see you then."

And then she left me.

After the Session

That night, I dreamed of meeting Mae.

It wasn't an unusual dream. It was definitely one I had more often than the one where CPS took me away from my mother for the first time.

Third year in college.

I was busting my ass in class during the day and working back of house in a restaurant in the afternoons. Then I stayed up most of the night studying. I spent almost all of my time in a half-sleep fog, going through the motions, trying to convince myself that it would all be worth it one day, but not quite believing it.

It was that year that I had (alright maybe a little foolishly) taken a women's studies class. Maybe partly because I thought it would be a great place to meet some really smart, really sexually confident women. Which, it was. It also turned out to be one of my favorite subjects after I got over the raised brows and eye rolls I got for the first few classes.

It was in that class that I met Natalie.

Natalie was everything I had ever wanted in a woman. Smart. Sharp-tongued. Sure of herself. An animal in fucking bed, teaching me more than a few things those first few months. She was also gorgeous. Tall. Thin, but womanly. Long blonde hair. Sharp facial features. Green eyes. She was the biggest ball buster I ever met and constantly kept me on my toes.

Perfect. Or at least I was convinced of that at the time.

It was four weeks in when I went to her apartment for the first time.

That was how I met Mae.

Mae was two years younger than me and Natalie.

And opposite to her in almost every way.

Smaller. She was so short she was almost childish, but also curvy enough that you knew exactly how much of a woman she really was. She was red haired (the deep auburn kind), freckled, and blue-eyed. She was smart, but in a more studied, bookish way. In all the time I knew her, I never knew her to have a harsh word. She was always backing away from an argument, always compromising her opinion for the person's with more passion.

The longer I dated Natalie, the more time I spent with Mae. It was partly because she was always around- never one to party or even just go hang out and catch a movie or live music. So on the nights where Nat had classes, I would stay in her apartment, bent over my books, and try to force Mae out of her shell a little bit.

It was six months before I learned why she flinched when I got too close.

"You don't have to tell me if you don't want to," I said, watching her chew on her lip, her feet up on the couch, her arm wrapped around her legs.

"If you're going to be a shrink, you're not going to be able to give in that easily," she said, giving me a small smile.

89

"Alright, fine," I said, smiling. "Tell me why you're uncomfortable when I get close to you."

A part of me knew. Or, at least, suspected. Watching her eyes fall from mine as she took a shaky breath, yeah, it confirmed it. "My first week on campus," she started, her voice small. "I went to a party. I got drunk for the first time. And I..." she sighed, pausing. "I don't know honestly. I woke up in a bed with someone and... we had sex. Or maybe I was raped. I don't even know. I remember spending time with him. I even remember going to his bedroom. After that, it's blurry." She was silent for long enough for me to think she wasn't going to go on. "That was my first time," she said and my heart broke for her. "It was my first time and I still don't know if I lost it willingly or not."

"Christ," I said, shaking my head, wanting to go over to her and give her a hug, but knowing she would never allow that. "I'm sorry that happened to you, honey," I said instead.

"Happens to girls everyday," she hedged, trying to turn my attention away from her.

"Yeah," I said, nodding. "I'm sorry that it happens to them too. But that happening to them doesn't make whatever happened to you any less important. And just so you know," I went on, making my words a little more firm, "if for any reason... drugs or being drunk or whatever... you don't remember it happening, it shouldn't have happened at all. You couldn't consent like that. Whatever did happen was *wrong*, Mae. And that wasn't your fault. It was *his* fault. So don't go taking on the blame." I paused, gentling my tone again, "Have you... talked to anyone about this?"

She looked up, right into my eyes, "Just you."

"Do you think you can, maybe, keep talking to me about it? Not right now," I said, watching her. "But... whenever you need to talk about it. I'm a good listener."

"You won't tell Nat?" she asked, looking anxious.

"I won't tell anyone unless you want me to."

She let out her held breath, nodding a little. "Okay."

"Okay," I said back, letting the subject drop and going back to my books.

But from then on, when she needed to, she talked to me.

She talked about what she remembered from that night. She talked about how she felt that next morning. How she kept it from Natalie when she got back to their apartment and Nat asked some questions. She told me about the trip to the clinic she made to get checked up a few weeks later. She told me how she didn't like leaving her apartment anymore because she was afraid she would cross paths with the guy from the party again.

Then she told me that she never

ever

wanted to have sex again.

Fifth Session

By the time she walked into my office Thursday night, I had managed to work myself into a million untangle-able knots. About her. About what I felt like was happening. About me. About why I was feeling the things I was. About if it was just my past coming up to haunt me. About my fucking career- the one thing that I had in my life that mattered. My livelihood. My passion. It was the thing that was being threatened every single time she graced my office with her presence.

I was tense. Every nerve was on edge. A muscle was ticking in my jaw.

The door opened and Ava walked in dressed head to toe in black, turning to lock the door behind her.

"Ava," I said, careful to not call her a pet name at first greeting, knowing that was a habit I had to break.

"Hey," she said back, her voice wavering.

My mind cleared enough to take in that she was still in the doorway. She was as tense as I was. That anxiety was practically sparking off her skin.

"You look like you're ready to bolt."

"Yeah."

"Care to tell me why?"

A strange pained look passed over her face, but she quickly pushed it away and a brow rose instead. "I don't know. Care to tell me why you're so tense?"

Ha.

Well then.

She had me there.

And damn if it wasn't sexy as hell that she was calling me out on my shit.

"That was... snippy," I said, fighting a smile.

"Yes. I have feelings other than anxiety you know," she said, lifting her chin defiantly. But it was all bluster. She was covering something else, an emotion more delicate than anger.

"I'm getting a picture," I said, letting myself smile. I felt some of the tension leaving my body, enjoying getting to see Ava in another new light. And fuck if she didn't look great in it too. "Jake on your nerves again?" I asked.

"Jake's been great actually," she said, surprising me, but I was glad for it too.

"Work getting to you?" I tried.

"I took off yesterday. And it was my manager's birthday today so all we did was eat cake and gab." That was more information than she normally offered. And yet, she wasn't telling me anything.

"You took off yesterday? Were you sick?"

She looked like she might roll her eyes at me, like I was trying her patience. In the end, she just exhaled. "No. I just wanted a day off."

"What did you do?" I asked, wondering if it meant something that she was still in the doorway. I knew why I was still behind the desk. I needed to keep some literal space between us or I was never going to be able to keep the metaphorical space I needed from her.

"I ate enough gelato to feed a small village and watched TV with Jake."

She liked gelato. Not normal ice cream. Gelato. It was something I felt glad knowing. Which made no sense. Because it was something that I had no reason to want to know about a client. A patient.

"Sounds like a good day."

"It was much needed," she agreed on a small nod.

Alright. That was enough.

"Are you going to stand in the doorway all night?"

"Are you going to stand behind the desk all night?" she countered, her tone sharp and I wanted to strip her down and fuck her right where she was standing. Was there anything hotter than a woman who could dish it out a little?

"Alright, smartass," I smiled as I moved toward my office door, "let's go get a drink."

I heard her following behind me as I went to make drinks. Beside me, at the stereo, she jabbed her finger at the screen harder than necessary. Then, a few seconds later, ear-piercing metal screamed through the speakers.

I lifted a brow, handing her a drink and watched her throw it back in one shot. I did the same. I had a feeling I was going to need it.

"I get it," I said, taking her drink and setting it aside. "You're in a mood." I moved to the stereo and flipped through the playlists. "But let's listen to something a little more appropriate for the session," I said, hitting a sensual r&b playlist. "You haven't asked what tonight's session is yet."

"I know."

"Do you want to know?" I asked, my brows drawing together in confusion. Everything about her was off. She wasn't making any kind of sense.

She shrugged. "Sure."

Sure? *Sure?* What the fuck was going on with her?

She wanted to play that game? I could play. And I could win.

So I went and laid down the royal flush.

"I am going to go down on you. And you are going to go down on me." Unfortunately, I didn't get the response I was looking for- meaning a genuine Ava one. No. I got a bit of wide eye, a bit of parted lips, but then... nothing. "Do you know what that means?"

"Yes."

"Oral sex," I clarified.

"I'm aware."

Jesus Christ.

"Okay. Enough," I clipped. "What's the matter?"

"I'm fine."

"No... you're not."

"Is that your... *professional* opinion?"

Fucking hell.

If there was one thing I didn't want thrown in my face that night, that was it.

"Are you having problems with this situation?"

Something flashed again. "I think things are going pretty well."

"That's not what I asked, Ava. I want..." I wanted a lot of god damn things I could never fucking have was what I wanted. "Oh, fuck talking..." I growled, grabbing her roughly and crashing my lips down on hers.

Gone was Chase, the doctor. Or Chase, the surrogate.

It was just fucking me. Just me and what I wanted. Hard. Rough. Consuming. Demanding. My teeth bit her lip until she gasped so my tongue could slip inside to claim hers. My hands went under her sweater up her back. Then they moved around to the front. Up her belly. Over her bra, squeezing to the point of pain before slipping my hands inside the cups to pinch and twist her nipples.

I made her walls fall down.

I made her let me *fucking in*.

Then and only then did I pull away.

"There. That's better," I said, taking in her heavy-lidded cloudy eyes, her flushed cheeks, her beard-burnt skin, her swollen lips. The shield was gone. I had my girl back.

Jesus fuck.

She wasn't *my* anything.

"Don't think you can..." she started, her tone angry. But I wasn't letting her go there. I grabbed her sweater, pulling it up roughly, making her stop talking. "Listen..." she started, shirt gone, glaring at me.

"Nope," I said, shrugging.

"What?" she asked, looking shocked.

Good. Shocked was good. Angry was good. Turned on was good. Anything other than the closed down mask she was wearing before was good.

"No. I'm not going to listen. I am going to take the rest of your clothes off and bury my face in your pussy until you are screaming so loud you forget all about being in this pissy ass mood."

Not a minute after the words left my mouth, she was out of her bra. And pants. And panties.

"Much better," I said, raking my eyes over her body, wanting to memorize every last inch. "Get on the bed."

"You're still..." she started, waving a hand toward my clothes.

Then I was out of them. Except for my boxer briefs.

"Now get on the bed," I told her, my tone brooking no god damn further argument.

She got on the bed.

I moved to the foot of the bed, grabbing her and dragging her down toward the edge. I grabbed her ankles, putting them on my shoulders, making her legs spread wide for me so I could look at her pussy.

And it was drenched.

Fuck me.

"Chase..." she started to object, squirming a little under my inspection.

"Shh," I said, not wanting to have to ruin the moment. She was spread before me. For the moment, she was fucking *mine*. And I took damn good care of what was mine. So I dipped my head and I ran my tongue up the crease of her pussy, letting her taste consume my senses as she moaned. I ate her like my fucking life depended on it- like it was the last time I would get to taste a pussy- like I needed to make it good enough to last a lifetime.

I waited until she was writhing, clutching the sheets, groaning until I curled my tongue and slipped it inside her.

"Oh my god," she cried, her hands slamming down on my head, holding me tight to her like she was worried I would stop. I never wanted to stop. So I thrust fast, unrelenting, fucking her with with my tongue until her whimpers and moans became begs for release.

"Chase... please... please...."

Her pussy was tight around my tongue. She was going to come. I slid my tongue up her cleft and pressed it hard against her clit.

Then all there was in the world was her crying out my name over and over as she came.

"Fuck baby," I said, lifting my head to look at her. Come drunk, her only response was to pat the back of my head. "Hmm," I said, looking back down at her pussy. "I don't think that quite cut it," I teased.

"Chase, I can't..." she started to object.

"Well, we'll just see about that, won't we?"

And then we did.

And she totally could.

And she screamed loud enough to forget about her pissy ass mood.

"You taste so sweet," I told her, moving beside her and pulling her onto my chest. Don't ask me why. That was just where I always seemed to want her. It was where she belonged.

God.

I needed to stop thinking shit like that.

She settled into me, her body going soft, her breathing becoming even.

"You okay?" I asked a while later, reminding myself I had a fucking job to do. That job included making sure she wasn't freaking out about my face between her legs.

"Mmmhmmm," the sound vibrated through her.

"Little come-drunk, huh?" I asked, feeling a little (okay pretty damn) proud of myself.

"What?" she asked, tilting her head up to look at me.

"Come drunk. Orgasm drunk," I explained, watching as the realization made her face light up and had her giggling.

She put her head back down on my chest. "I guess."

"You handled that a lot better than I thought you would."

"Did you expect me to start yelling and push you off?"

"Maybe," I mused. "Maybe something not so dramatic. I didn't think you would just... enjoy yourself."

"I enjoyed... you," she said shyly.

Christ.

She was so fucking sweet.

"That's sweet," I said, leaning down and kissing her head. "God, you're like a teensy little oven," I complained, kicking off the sheets for some cool air because there was no way I wanted her to move off of me.

Her gaze went down to where my cock was still straining hard through my underwear. Then, ever so slowly, her hand started moving downward.

"Babe," I said, grabbing her wrist, not wanting her to think she had to do anything just because I took care of her. "It's okay. We have all night. You don't need to..."

"But I want to," she said, pushing up on my chest so she could look down at me.

"Fuck me," I sighed, bringing a hand up to the side of her face. I knew I needed to bite my tongue, but I didn't.

98

"You're perfect just how you are, okay? Don't let anyone try to convince you otherwise. Not even yourself."

She gave me a small smile before moving across my body to straddle me. Her head started to move down to kiss my chest, but I grabbed her to stop her. "Wait," I said, watching her. "Let a man enjoy the view for a second," I said, not bothering to hide the smile as I let my hands glide over her body. My hands stopped at her breasts, my fingers teasing across her nipples. "Perfect."

Then she moved down, kissing a trail across my chest, my stomach, lower. Her hands went to my underwear and slipped them down, letting my cock out.

Then... nothing.

Shit.

She wasn't ready.

"Ava..." I broke in, my tone soothing, relaxed, patient. Like my balls didn't feel like they were in a vise grip. Because that didn't matter. Well, it didn't matter as much as her comfort level did anyway.

"Let a *woman* enjoy the view for a second," she said, smiling and I felt a laugh burst from my chest.

Then her hand grabbed me and stroked down to the hilt and the laughter died. She leaned down, twirling her tongue around the head, licking off the precum and sending a shudder through my body as my hand grabbed at her hair. Her mouth moved to close around me tight, sucking me in, moving downward slowly until I felt the head push up against the back of her throat.

"Holy... *fuck...* Ava..."

Then her eyes drifted up to mine and it was the hottest fucking thing I had ever seen. She kept her gaze on me as she started working my cock with her mouth. It wasn't expert. It wasn't evident of practice. It wasn't *perfect*. But it was passionate. It was full of the genuine desire to please. And that *made* it perfect.

So I didn't offer any advice. I didn't try to help her learn to do it like a pro. I just enjoyed her. Her mouth on my shaft. Her tongue over my head. Her hand at my balls. All of it.

"Ava," I warned, knowing I was seconds from popping. "I'm gonna come. If you don't want..."

But she did want.

She wanted me to come.

Her tongue slid over the head one last time then she sucked me deep and I came down her throat. Hard. Harder than I could ever recall coming before. She sucked it up greedily, licking every bit of moisture off my cock before kissing her way back up to my neck.

She moved to lay her head on my chest where she belonged but my hands went out to grab her, to cradle her face, wanting to make her understand even the tiniest bit of what that meant to me. "Ava..."

"I did good, didn't I?" she cut me off, an adorably self-satisfied smile on her face.

"No baby," I said, shaking my head. "That wasn't good. That was fucking phenomenal," I told her, running my hands over her cheeks, her lips. I couldn't get enough of touching her.

As I was watching her, something came over her face. Not like before. Something different. Something I didn't understand. But it was warm. It made her eyes soft. It made her light up the room.

Then she ducked her head, lying back down on my chest.

Before long, she was asleep.

I just held her, completely awake, staring at the ceiling until an hour passed. Until I got impatient. Until I got hard again.

Then I swatted her ass and she jerked awake. "What?" she grumbled, sounding annoyed.

"Nothin'," I said, smiling. "I just wanted you to wake up."

"What for?"

I felt a devilish grin split my face. "I'm going to taste you again."

Her head tilted to the side as she inspected me. "Why do I feel like there's a hitch?"

"This time you're going to ride my face." I saw the (expected) shock and denial overtake her face. "And at the same time, you're going to suck my cock again."

A flash of heat went into her eyes.

Like she wanted to do that again.

Like she was hungry for my cock.

Fuck, fuck me.

"Chase..."

"You don't like it, we stop. No questions asked. Let's give it a try, okay?"

"Okay."

Then we did, her straddling my head, her mouth on my cock while I sucked her clit until she screamed my name again.

Two AM. She was getting dressed. I was in my pants and buttoning my shirt. "I need to see you tomorrow."

"What?" she asked, looking confused.

"For the next session. Tomorrow," I clarified.

The next session was sex.

I was going to be *inside* her.

Then she was shaking her head no, dragging me out of my fantasy. "No? Why? What's the matter? Are you nervous? Because we should talk about it then, babe."

"No... I, ah, I have plans to go out with a coworker. Shay. She's... been pestering me and I finally agreed."

"That's great," I said, feeling like it was anything but. Feeling like there was a high possibility of her being dragged out on the town, being paraded in front of men. Other men. Other men who would take one look at her and drop to a knee.

But that wasn't my place. It wasn't my concern. At least, it couldn't be. I needed to get a grip. "Okay. Monday night. At seven."

Suddenly, that felt forever away.

After the Session

Friday brought with it an early day of work. No one wanted to see their shrink after work on payday. So I went to see Eddie's new apartment. It was, well, a step up from the last one which was a step up from a slum. It looked like he was genuinely trying to get his life back on track.

I would have been relieved.

If I wasn't spending all my time worried about Ava.

About how off the last session was.

About how shitty I felt when she left.

About the next session.

About it fucking all.

It was consuming me every waking moment.

"What's with you?" Eddie asked, hopping up onto his faded yellow kitchen counter.

I shook my head, trying to clear it. "Just got some shit on my mind," I hedged. I was already messing around with my professional boundaries. I didn't need to introduce violating patient/client privilege on top of it all.

Eddie's lips quirked up at one side, making a dimple etch into his cheek. "I know that look, man."

"What look?"

"That one. The one that says you got some chick on your mind."

If Eddie hadn't snorted, shot, and drank his early twenties away, he could have gone into something that put his ability to read people to use. Psychology, like me. Law enforcement. Military.

"Yeah," I admitted, figuring it was safe to at least admit I was having a problem with a woman so long as I didn't let on what the *real* problem was.

At this, Eddie threw his head back and laughed. It had been so long since I had witnessed that sight, that I just stood there and watched. "Shit. I've known you for over twenty years, Chase. Never knew you to have woman trouble. Too many women wanting on your dick trouble? Sure. But not the pain in the ass shit like the rest of us deal with." He shook his head. "So what's the deal?"

I ran a hand down the scruff on my face. "Want her. Can't have her."

Eddie's brows drew together. "You? *You* can't have her? What is she married or something?"

She might as well have been. "No. Just... can't have her," I shrugged.

Then up went Eddie's brows and I knew I should have kept my fucking mouth shut. "Shit... you caught feelings for a fucking patient, man? Jesus. You're so fucked."

That about covered it.

My phone rang late, screaming from the table beside the front door, making me stumble around my apartment half-awake, having fallen asleep on my couch. It stopped ringing by the time I got there and noticed the missed call was from Ava's cell.

Just as I was swiping to call her back, the indicator light told me I had a message.

"I don't care what Dr. Bowler says," she started, her words a little slow. Drunk. She was drunk. I found myself smiling as I listened, wondering what the hell Dr. Bowler had told her. "It feels real. And you can be as mea..." Mean? She thought I had been mean to her? My thoughts cleared though when her sentence cut off with, "Stop pawing at me!" My heart skidded into overdrive. Pawing at her? Someone was pawing at her? Someone she *didn't want to paw at her* was pawing at her? "I am talking to Chase's machine. Leave me alone," she added, attempting stern and failing because whoever the fuck the guy was that she was with just laughed. *Laughed.* That son of a ...

"So... anyway, Chase. I don't care if it's fake, you know?" Fake? What was fake? "It's okay. I'll deal with that... okay buddy!" she started, angrier and I heard the distinct sound of a slap. "Get off my couch. Off. Get off!" My. Get off *my* couch. She was at home. I was in my shoes and grabbing my keys by the time she spoke again. "You ruined my message!" she whined. And then nothing. The line went dead.

Fuck.

Fuck fuck fuck.

It would take me at least ten minutes to get to her place.

Anything could happen to her in ten minutes.

I tore up her staircase twelve minutes later, hearing the music and voices as I rounded the corner to her apartment. They were having some kind of party. That didn't mean she was safe. If some asshole persuaded her into the bedroom or the bathroom...

And her clueless fucking roommate was probably too busy skirt chasing to keep an eye on her.

Fuck fuck fuck.

I threw open the door, my eyes moving around the room frantically. Then I saw the back of her head sitting on the couch with some ex-frat looking guy with her.

"I don't think I work that way..." she told him, sounding confused.

"Oh, baby. I can *make* you work that way," he offered and I wanted to knock all of his teeth down his fucking throat.

"You're not allowed to call me that," she told him as I came around the couch.

"Why not?"

"Because Chase calls me that," she said, stopping me dead and kicking the air out of me.

"Who the hell is Chase?"

"I am," I said, my words sounding hard even to my own ears.

Ava's head turned in my direction, looking confused for a second before her face split into a huge (albeit super drunk) grin. "It's Chase!" she declared loudly, pointing at me. And fuck if I didn't want to kiss her silly. "You're here!"

I felt my lips turn up slightly, trying to push my anger at the idiot beside her away when I was addressing her. "Yeah, baby." Then I turned to look at the guy, ready to just tell him to get lost when I saw he had put his hand on her again. On her thigh. Way too far up to be appropriate. "Get your hands off of her," I hissed, my voice low. "Take a look at her. Does she really seem like she is in any condition to consent?"

"She's fine, man," he said, rolling his eyes. "Who the hell are you?"

"He's Chase!" Ava chimed in, cheery as hell and I had to fight to keep my eyes off of her.

"Get. Lost." I enunciated carefully as I reached down, grabbed him by the front of his shirt, and dragged him onto his feet.

"Alright. Alright. Fuck. She ain't worth all this trouble."

"Hey!" Ava yelled, lowering her eyes at him like she was angry.

I took a deep breath, pushing the worry and anger aside, before I looked back at her again. And she looked beautiful. She was in a tight electric blue dress that fit her like a glove, her hair straighter than usual, makeup on her eyes, making them pop even more than they already did. Jesus. "So," I sighed. "did you have a fun night?"

"I had a *lot* to drink," she declared easily.

"Seems like it," I agreed, moving into the empty space beside her. "So where is your friend?"

"Shay?" she asked.

"Yes, Shay." Why the hell wasn't she watching out for her friend? Especially when said friend was obviously a lightweight.

"Oh. Look for the most beautiful girl in the room. That's her."

"I'm looking at the most beautiful girl in the room," I told her, my hand moving out to stroke her silky hair though I knew I should have been hightailing it out of there.

Her brows drew together slightly. "You need to stop saying things like that."

"Why?" I asked, knowing I was taking advantage of her with her inhibitions down. But, hell, I wanted to know what was going on in that pretty little head of hers.

"Because I like it," she said easily.

"Isn't that even more reason that I should say it?" I asked, liking it way too much that she liked what I said to her. I reached out, grabbing her legs and pulled them over my lap.

"I don't know," she said, sounding genuinely confused. "I feel like no."

"Hey," a woman's voice cut in and I looked up to find a gorgeous dark skinned woman with long dreads and a face that could grace a catwalk standing near the coffee table. "She's wasted. Back off," she said in a tone that brooked no argument and I found myself smiling at her.

"That's Ava's..." Jake started, walking up, fumbling for a cover for what I was, "Friend," he went with, putting an arm around Shay. "It's fine. She's fine..." he said, leading her away.

"I like Shay," I told the top of Ava's head.

"She's good people," Ava said, sounding sleepy as she scooted closer, resting her face on my chest like I liked.

It was my only chance.

"Who is Dr. Bowler babe?" I went with, knowing she was one of her shrinks. It was in her paperwork.

"She's my shrink. My other shrink. She's good people too. Even if she's right."

"Right about what?"

"But I think she might be wrong. But maybe not. That's how it works, I guess."

"How what works?"

She just shook her head though, taking a deep breath and snuggling closer. My arm went around her, pulling her close. "This is my spot," she declared, tapping my chest with her hand.

Her spot.

Fuck.

Fuck yeah it was.

God damn it.

My other arm went around her too and I kissed the top of her head, not wanting to kill the moment with things like proper code of conduct. In that moment, I wasn't her doctor. She wasn't my patient. We were just two people.

"Yeah, baby, it is," I agreed.

"Safest place in the world," she said, drifting off to sleep.

Safest place in the world.

She thought my chest was the safest place in the world. Fuck me.

Then I felt it. Strong. Sure. More sure than I had ever felt about anything in my life.

I loved her.

And it was nothing like I had thought.

It wasn't like sunshine. It wasn't like warmth.

No.

It was just an easy feeling.

It was knowing that given the choice between spending my night with her asleep on my chest or doing anything else in the world, I would choose her every single time.

Without thinking.

Easy.

What the fuck was I supposed to do now?

I held her to me, stroking up and down her back, through her hair, over her cheek, as the party dwindled down around us and all that was left was Shay and Jake. The former came over, dropped down on the coffee table right in front of me, her brown eyes seeming to x-ray right into my soul.

"So, you're really attractive," she said, ripping a surprised laugh from my chest.

"Thanks."

"I mean the tall, dark, scruffy, sexy thing is really working for you."

"Thanks again," I said, smiling. She would be good for Ava. Bold. Confident. Some of it could eventually, little by little, rub off on her.

"Now there's something I know about really attractive, tall, dark, scruffy, sexy men."

"What's that?" I asked, Ava stirring against me and my arms instinctively tightened around her.

"They tend to trample shy and sweet girls with fragile hearts."

"I have no intentions of trampling Ava," I said honestly.

"Maybe not, but that doesn't mean you won't. So let me just get this straight *right fucking now*," she said, her tone going from light and almost flirtatious to deep and stern in an instant. "You hurt my girl here, I am going to buy a cactus, find you, and shove it up your ass," she said in a way that I didn't doubt her for a second. "'Kay?"

Again, I laughed. "I like you, Shay," I told her honestly. Had I met her two weeks earlier, she would have been just my type.

"I like me too. And I like my girl. So toe the line and you won't have reason to *dis*like me."

"Jesus Christ, Shay," Jake broke in, sounding frustrated. "Leave the man alone."

"I am just making it clear where things stand. Something I am assuming your ass forgot to do."

"You don't underst..." Jake's eyes went to me and he sighed. "Whatever. I don't want to fucking argue over this. You're killing my buzz."

"You should hit the sack anyway. Alone," she clarified with a pointed look.

"Yeah. Okay, Mom."

"Just saying... six o'clock is going to come before you know it."

"I don't get up at six o'clock."

"Well," she said, slapping her hands down on her thighs before standing, "tomorrow you do."

"Why the fuck would I do that?"

"Because you are helping me clean this apartment before Ava gets up."

"Like hell I..."

"Go to fucking bed," she said again, firmer. And damn if Jake didn't turn and go back to bed.

"See you in the morning, Dark and Sexy," Shay said, not looking at me as she made her way to, what I assumed was Ava's bedroom. "I'm making breakfast."

I was awake for a long time, trying to figure out how to get myself out of such a clusterfuck of a situation. I came up with nothing. Because Ava *needed* me. But she needed me to be Dr. Chase Hudson. She needed to have those boundaries so she could let down her guards and learn to be comfortable with men. She needed me in a professional capacity. She didn't need me pining for her. Admitting my feelings for her. She didn't need that pressure. That confusion.

She fucking needed me to get my shit together.

So that was what I needed to do.

The next morning.

After breakfast.

True to her word, Shay was up and showered in a pair of pajama pants and a tank top at six in the morning, banging down Jake's door until he opened and stepped out, bleary-eyed, but surprisingly following her orders.

Once the apartment was cleaned, Shay and Jake moved into the kitchen, working side by side to make breakfast and I got the distinct impression that something was brewing there. It was in the playful banter. In the arguing. In the long stares when the other wasn't looking.

Those two were going to have something going on. Soon.

I wondered how Ava would handle that.

As if on cue, Ava groaned, her eyes opening to squint at the bright morning light.

"Hey there, sleeping beauty."

She shot up, body going tense, tilting her head to look at me. "Chase?"

"Yeah, babe," I said, registering the pain in her brown eyes.

111

Then those eyes went wide as she, I imagined, tried to go over the events of the night. "Oh, god..." she said, burying her face in her hands. "Please tell me I didn't say anything stupid."

"No, babe. You fell asleep almost as soon as I got here."

She was silent a moment, still trying to piece the parts of the night together. "Why did you come?"

"I heard you yelling at someone to stop touching you. He didn't seem to get the message. So I just wanted to make sure you were okay. If I had known what a guard dog Shay is, I wouldn't have been so worried."

"Hey, us gals got to stick together," Shay called from the kitchen, waving a spatula.

Her head snapped in the direction of Shay's voice and her mouth fell slightly open. "Okay. I think I woke up in some different dimension," she said, looking around the clean apartment like it didn't make sense.

"Jake and I got up early to clean for you. I know you like things neat."

"That was really sweet," Ava said, sounding almost emotional. Like she never expected anyone to do anything nice for her. She probably didn't. "Wait. Did you say *Jake* got up early and *cleaned*?"

"Yeah," Shay said, shrugging.

"Did you have him at gunpoint?"

"Girl, all you need to handle a man like him is a sharp tongue and a withering stare. Boy got sisters. He's trained to obey."

"She's not wrong," Jake said, giving me a 'what can 'ya do' look.

"Then how come you never do what I ask?" Ava countered, lowering her eyes at him.

"Because," Shay answered. "You can't ask. You tell."

"I'll have to keep that in mind," Ava said, then as if suddenly realizing what position we were in, moved away from me, reaching to pull down the hem of her dress which had ridden up high on her thigh. "Alright. I need to go get some less... binding clothes," she said, getting off of me and quickly making her way to her room.

"You looking to talk to her," Shay broke in, not even looking up, "better go now before she gets herself all thinking on shit."

With that, I got up off the couch and made my way into her bedroom to find her in her closet.

"I'll have the dress cleaned for you and bring it to work on Monday," she said, obviously expecting Shay.

She turned slowly at my silence. "Hey baby."

"Hey," she said hesitantly, grabbing a towel and piling it with her clothes.

"Turn around," I said, making my way toward her.

Her eyes flashed with desire and she slowly turned around, giving me a glorious view of the heart-shaped cut out in the back of her dress. My fingers went out and stroked the exposed skin and she shivered. "You look so sexy in this dress," I told her.

"Thank you," she said, accepting the compliment easily. Which was a step in the right direction.

My hands went to her shoulders, pressing into the knotted muscles she had from sleeping sitting up all night. She sank back into me, her head tilting to the side, a low groan escaping her lips. And, fuck, I couldn't help myself.

I leaned forward, tracking down her neck with my lips as her breath got more and more unsteady, as a tremble moved through her body.

"Okay. You should stop that," she said weakly.

"Why? Are you getting wet for me baby?" I asked, half teasing.

She shocked the shit out of me when she answered, "Yes."

"Good," I murmured, moving up to nibble her earlobe. "I want you thinking about me every minute until Monday night. And every time you think of me, I want you to be wet."

There was a heavy silence and I knew my words were pushing her further and further toward the edge. "Think you can do that for me?"

"Yes."

"Good. And when you get to my office," I said, my nose moving across her neck, "you are going to be wearing a dress."

"Why?"

"Because I am going to push you up against the wall, rip off your panties, lift up your skirt, and lick your clit until you are begging for release."

She swallowed hard. "Anything else?"

God, she was going to kill me.

"You're not allowed to touch yourself at all until then."

Not even a hesitation before, "Okay."

"Good girl," I praised her, then stepped away before I couldn't control myself anymore. "Now go get showered. Shay and Jake are almost done with breakfast."

I walked out before she could say anything else, moving out toward the kitchen to where Jake was already holding out a coffee cup toward me.

"Talk go well?" Shay asked, scooping breakfast potatoes onto four plates.

"I guess," I said, looking at Jake.

"You know... she's not as weak as everyone thinks she is," Shay said, piling pancakes next to the potatoes. "Don't go walking on eggshells around her. She can put up with me being the badass bitch I am, and Jake being the pain in the ass jerk he is," she said, her words almost affectionate when she raised a brow at Jake as if daring him to defend himself, "then she can put up with you being your normal alpha self."

"My normal alpha self?" I asked, raising a brow, wondering how the hell she could read me so easily.

Her gaze met mine and her brow lifted in challenge. "You know what I mean. I'm just saying. You ain't doin' her or you no favors by hiding that. Honestly, I think she would eat that right up."

"We are not having this conversation," Jake broke in, looking uncomfortable.

"This guy fucks everything with legs capable of spreading and he thinks I'm being inappropriate," she said, handing me a container of orange juice and nodding toward the table. I took this as some kind of instruction to fill the glasses she had Jake set on the table. So I did.

Behind us, Ava's door opened and I heard another door close before the water in the shower came on.

Shay barked out orders (mostly at Jake) until Ava came out to join us, hesitating when she walked out, watching us laugh over something that Shay said.

I turned and smiled at her, patting the chair next to me.

She sat down, looking uncomfortable, her eyes red and small and I handed her two aspirin I had gotten out of a bottle on the kitchen counter.

"Eat," Shay told her. "And drink all that OJ or you're gonna feel like shit all day."

Everyone ate. Jake and Shay kept up the lion's share of the conversation, mostly by bickering, but it was playful enough that Ava came out of her shell enough to laugh or roll her eyes at them.

"So how did you two meet?" Shay asked, point blank.

Ava's fork clattered onto her plate and I felt a lump lodge into my throat. Both of us were silent for too long. And in the end, it was Jake who saved us. "Jesus Christ. Could you be any more nosy?" he asked, leading them to spend the next five minutes having a heated argument. Which Shay won. Naturally. Jake gave me a sheepish smile and I nodded my chin to him in thanks as I squeezed Ava's knee under the table.

I left an hour later, stomach full to bursting and somehow more hollow than I had ever felt in my life.

In two days, I would be having sex with the only woman I ever really loved.

And then in just four more sessions, I would have to say goodbye to her.

For good.

Sixth Session

Ever try to concentrate on work when you have something amazing planned for after hours? Amplify that by about a thousand and you'd have some idea how I felt all day Monday.

By the time the door opened, I was in knots. Both in good and bad ways.

Because I couldn't wait to touch her. To taste her. To be inside her. To show her all the magnificent ways her body could feel. I wanted to show her that she could enjoy herself. I wanted to show her how she could enjoy me.

But also... in no time at all, she would be gone. She would move on enjoying herself. Then, one day, she would go onto enjoying other men.

I was tucking the test results I had meant to give to her five sessions ago into my pocket before looking up and... fuck.

I thought I liked the blue dress. The white one she was wearing put it to shame. Form fitting, a little low cut, short on the thigh. Verging on risqué, but the color somehow kept it from being over the top sexual. It looked... sweet almost... Christ... virginal. Did she do that on purpose? Was it a message? That this, for her, felt like the first time since all previous times had been so awful for her?

"Oh, baby," I said, tilting my head and looking at her in a way that I was almost surprised her dress didn't catch fire from the heat.

She shifted her feet slightly, tucking her hair behind her ear. "I, ah, believe I was promised something that involved being... um... pushed against a wall," she fumbled. But the stammer only proved to be all the more endearing.

I felt the smile creep up on my face. "That you were," I agreed, crossing the floor, grabbing her by the back of her neck, and pressing my lips to hers, kissing her with every last drop of hope and frustration I felt. I slammed her back against the wall, my tongue slipping into her mouth as my hand slid between her soft thighs, finding her clit through her panties and stroking. "So wet," I said against her lips.

"Chase..."

Whatever she was about to say was silenced by my ripping her panties off and lowering myself down on the floor before her. I looked up at her as I slowly inched up her skirt until it was bunched around her belly.

"Tell me it's for me."

"Always," she said without hesitation. "It's always for you."

"Fuck, baby," I groaned, grabbing her leg and placing it over my shoulder, not able to wait another second as I traced my tongue up her slick pussy until I found her clit and worked it until she was moaning, writhing, pulling my hair. Until she was almost there. Almost. Just when she was about to come, I pulled back.

"Chase..." she groaned, reaching for me as I looked up at her.

"Don't worry, baby. I am going to make you come tonight. Just not yet. First," I said, taking my feet and reaching for her hand, "we need to go into the other room."

I made drinks.

She put on blues.

Then I led her over toward the sectional, watching her nervously sip from her martini. She might have come in attempting confidence, but it was a show. She was nervous. I hadn't expected anything else. That was why we were going to take it slow. I was going to try to put her at ease... before anything happened.

The last thing in the fucking world I wanted to be was another of her regrets.

"I figured maybe tonight we should do some talking first."

"Okay," she said, not meeting my gaze.

"First," I went on, putting my drink down and pulling the paperwork out of my pocket and handing it to her. "I should have given it to you a while ago. But I kept forgetting."

She unfolded the pages of my latest STD check, dated the day of the introductory meeting. All, of course, negative. But she needed to have it. She needed to know she was safe.

"I wanted you to feel completely comfortable with me. We will be using condoms, of course, but this was just for your peace of mind."

"Okay," she said, putting the papers down behind her. "Thanks," she said, addressing the hands she was wringing in her lap.

"I know you're nervous. Talk to me, babe."

"I don't know what to say," she shrugged, her voice a strained whisper.

"Say anything. Say that you're nervous. Say why. Just... talk."

"I'm nervous."

"Okay," I said, letting my hand land on her thigh.

"This is the thing I am most insecure about."

"What makes you so insecure? That you can't enjoy it? That you're worried about being a disappointment?"

"Both," she admitted quietly.

I felt myself nod though she wasn't watching me and let both of my hands land on top of hers. "Ava, nothing you could ever do would disappoint me. And I promise you that, no matter what happens, I will show you that you can enjoy it. No matter how long it takes." I added emphasis by squeezing her hands. "Okay?"

"Okay," she said, her gaze still lowered.

"Look at me," I demanded and waited for her deep brown eyes to find me- a little wide, a little scared, but trusting. "Do you believe me?"

"Yes."

"Good. Then come here," I said, sitting back and tapping my chest. Her spot. Her safest place in the world. The place I always wanted her to be. The place that soon, she would never rest on again.

She flew at me and my arms wrapped her up tight as I took a deep breath. "So let's talk about sex."

"Okay."

"In the past, have you ever had an orgasm through intercourse?"

"No."

"Ever been close?"

"No."

"Can you tell me what sex has been like for you in the past?"

"Terrible," she admitted surprisingly quickly. "As soon as clothes start coming off, the anxiety builds."

"And when someone has their hands on you, how do you feel?"

"Like I want to scrape off my skin," she said with conviction.

Poor fucking girl. I wanted to track down all the guys she had been with before and wring their necks for making her feel that way for even a second.

"Do you know why?"

"No. I mean, yes and no. I think the anxiety just makes me so uncomfortable and then angry because I can't control it that the touching feels wrong. And it hurts instead of feels good."

My cheek went down on the top of her head, not wanting to ask but knowing I had to. "And what about when they are inside of you?"

"I feel nothing," she said, her body going rigid.

"Nothing? Not even the skin crawling sensation?"

"I mean... the first time..."

"When you lost your virginity," I supplied, knowing she was struggling.

"Yeah..."

"That hurt," I added.

"Yes. A lot. I got sick."

"Okay," I said, squeezing her tight. "And since then... just numbness."

"Pretty much. Sometimes I can quiet the anxiety enough to feel, but just for like a couple seconds because it doesn't..." she trailed off, shaking her head.

"Because you were stressed out so you weren't turned on and it felt rough and uncomfortable," I cringed at the very idea, but pressed on. "And then the anxiety came back. Stronger."

"Yes."

"Alright," I said, kissing her soft hair. "Thank you for sharing that. That is helpful." My hands moved to rub her back lazily. "I'm sorry it's always been like that for you."

"It's okay."

"No, it's not," I corrected, shaking my head. "Baby," I said, moving back so I could look at her. "It's not okay. That should never have happened. Those guys..." I paused, swallowing the anger, "they should have seen that you were

121

struggling and they should have stopped and tried to help you through it."

"Not all guys are like you, Chase."

"No but they should fucking try to be," I growled, forcing myself to tamp down the anger. My hand moved to the side of her face and it evaporated. "Look, at any point tonight you feel anxious, you tell me. This isn't like the past when I told you that you should power through it and only push me away when you couldn't take it anymore. This is different. If you get above a four on that scale, you tell me. And if you don't feel like you can say it, all you have to do is say the word 'red' and I'll stop. And I'll try to talk you down. If that doesn't work, we can be done for the night. I will *not* be upset. I will *not* be disappointed. Understand?"

She nodded. "Yes."

"Good. What is the safe word?"

"Red."

"Good. Anything else?"

Her teeth moved to bite the inside of her cheek. There was something else. But she didn't want to say it. Or ask it.

"Ava... just ask."

She took a deep, steady breath. "How many..." she started.

I knew it was coming. Frankly, I was shocked she hadn't asked before. At the intro meeting even. Most wanted to know. Not because of jealousy or anything small and petty like that. But just pure curiosity.

She wanted to know how many surrogate clients I had.

"Twelve," I cut her off.

"Twelve?" she asked, brows drawing together like she was confused.

"Men are more likely to seek help for their dysfunction. Women, due to society sex standards and often their own upbringing, many women who are suffering simply won't seek help. Surrogacy is a very small part of my medical practice. I have been doing this for about a decade and I have only had about one surrogate patient a year."

She paused, thinking what I said over. "Okay."

"Okay," I repeated. "Come here," I said, pulling her face to mine. I kissed her like it was the first time. Like it was the last. Like it was all we would ever have. She shifted, moving to straddle my waist to get closer to me, her hands moving to cradle my face as she kissed me back with everything in her too.

My arms went around her as I stood. Her legs wrapped around me as I moved us toward the bed, turning so I could sit on the edge and settle her on top of me. My hands moved to slowly inch up her dress. Up her thighs. Ass. Stomach. Under her breasts. I waited for her to pull back so I could lift the material off of her body.

With the dress gone, and the panties ripped in my waiting room, she was gloriously naked above me. I looked over her, sucking in a deep, steadying breath. "Perfect," I said, my hands sliding up her stomach to cup her breasts then leaning forward to plant a kiss between them. "Thank you for sharing yourself with me."

Her hand moved to the back of my neck, toying with my hair. "Thank you for being so patient," she said, sliding back on my lap so she had access to my chest. Her hands moved between us to slide off my jacket then work my buttons. Once the sides slipped open, her hands went to the skin underneath, sending a shiver through my system. I let her explore until I felt on edge, then lifted her and placed her on the bed, standing to remove the rest of my clothes before climbing under the covers and pulling her to my side.

I let my hands whisper over her body, just getting her comfortable with the touch before I moved her onto her back and started kissing down her neck. Over her breasts. I moved to her nipples, licking and sucking them until they were hard and straining. Then I continued down her ribs, her belly, each of her thighs. Until she was whimpering, writhing, reaching for me and pulling me back up to her.

I reached behind me into the nightstand, grabbing a condom, and slipping it on. "This doesn't mean anything," I said, kissing her lips softly. "You can take all the time you need."

But she didn't need time.

I knew it when she reached for me, grabbing me and pulling until I moved over her, balancing my weight onto my forearms as her hands moved over my shoulders, my back, my ass. Her thighs parted and I slid into the space, my cock pressing hard against her pussy, already drenched, and rubbing against her clit.

"Chase..." she groaned, grinding her hips up into mine.

"You're sure?" I asked, my body tense, trying to hold myself back.

"Yes," she said, her tone airy. Needy.

Fuck me.

I leaned forward, kissing her until I felt the control slip back into place. I needed to go slow, to be gentle. No matter how much I wanted to slam forward and bury deep then fuck her until she screamed my name.

I shifted my hips until I was pressing against the entrance to her pussy, lifting my head to watch her face, to look for any sign of anxiety. But I saw none. So I pressed slowly forward, feeling her impossibly tight pussy squeeze my cock. Her mouth fell open slightly, her brows drawing together.

"You okay?" I asked, hoping to whatever god was listening that she said yes.

She nodded, spreading her legs wider, helping her body to acclimate as I kept inching in. I pushed to the hilt and her body jerked up, her head slamming into my arm.

"Ow," she groaned.

Shit.

"Okay," I said, stilling. "Baby, look at me," I said softly, waiting for her to draw a breath and lie back on the pillow. "I'm inside you," I told her, hoping it meant half of what it meant to me, to her. It meant fucking everything. I took a breath, trying to focus. "What's the number?" I asked, needing to know before we kept going.

"Three," she said a little breathlessly.

Thank god.

"I can work with three," I said, giving her a weak smile before taking her lips. Which she gave, happily. It wasn't long before her feet went flat on the mattress, her knees pressing into my sides as she moved her hips up toward me to try to get some release. I felt myself chuckle against her lips. Christ. She was ready. I raised my head and pulled slightly out then pressed back in. A whimper choked out of her throat. "So fucking tight," I groaned.

"So... big," she corrected a little shyly, but she was smiling.

I smiled down at her. "You ready?"

"Yes."

There was a tightening in my chest that I tried to forget as I drew halfway out of her then pressed fully back in, keeping the slow pace, wanting her first time really experiencing sex to be lovemaking- to be fulfilling emotionally and not just satiating physically.

I leaned down toward her ear, closing my eyes tight and breathing in her soft scent. "You're so beautiful," I told her, feeling her legs wrap around my back, her hands moving to grab my shoulders. Her hips started rising to meet my slow thrusts, circling them a little when I was buried deep.

"Oh my god... oh my god," she whimpered, her fingers digging into my back. And it was the sweetest fucking sound in the world.

"That's it baby," I said, lifting up so I could look down at her. I wanted to watch her fall apart. "Come for me. I want to feel your pussy grab me."

Then just like that, she came.

Her eyes went wide and her body stiffened for a moment right before her pussy started pulsating hard around me, dragging me to toward the edge with her.

"Chase!" she cried, burying her face in my neck and holding on tight as her body spasmed.

"Fuck. Beautiful." I pulled out then pressed back in, feeling my own orgasm course through me. "Ava... *fuck me...*" I groaned as I came.

My weight went down on her for a moment, my entire body spent, but she just wrapped me up tight as her body quaked through the aftershocks.

I sucked in a deep breath, putting myself back together, trying to pull against her hold. "Baby, let me look at you," I told her but she shook her head, pulling me tighter to her body. "I'll hold you, okay? Just let me look at you," I said and her arms slackened slightly so I could pull back. "Are you okay?" I asked and she immediately shook her head no, making my heart fly up into my throat. "No?"

Her eyes opened slowly. "Okay isn't even close to how you make me feel," she said, shocking me both with her words and with the intensity with which she said them.

"Oh, babe," I said, shaking my head like I didn't believe her as I rolled to my side and pulled her onto her side as well, my hand going to her face. "I'm glad you feel that way." And I was. Glad. Elated. So full of pride and amazement that it was a miracle I wasn't beaming from fucking ear to ear.

But then the look came.

The bad one. The pained, strained one that became a hollow mask, keeping my Ava from me.

"What's the matter?"

"Nothing," she lied. And it *was* a lie. A bold-faced lie. "I have to go to the bathroom," she said suddenly, moving toward the other side of the bed, taking the sheet with her as she shuffled toward the door and closed herself inside.

I sat up, dealing with the condom, trying to get my thoughts together. Trying to not worry too much about why the mask was back.

I waited.

Two minutes.

Five.

Getting more and more concerned.

Then I heard the shower water turn on and I stood up, moving toward the door. The sheet was discarded on the floor and the steam was already billowing out of the shower. I moved to the end and let myself in, taking a look at the soft skin of her back and ass, her hair a much darker blonde when it was wet.

"You should have told me you were taking a shower. I would have joined you," I said, moving in behind her, my hand landing right below her breasts and moving down her belly.

In front of me, she was stone. Stiff. Tense.

I moved in closer, knowing she took my presence as comfort, as my hand splayed her lower stomach.

"Red," she said, the word firm, almost harsh.

My hand froze then dropped as I took a step back.

Red.

She was using the safe word.

Fuck.

I *knew* it. I knew something was up.

God damn it.

"Ava, babe, what's wr..." I started, but she wasn't listening. No, she was climbing out of the shower, grabbing the only towel and haphazardly drying herself off as she made her way back into the bedroom.

By the time I followed (literally just seconds later) she was dragging her white dress awkwardly up her wet skin.

"Ava please talk to me..." I begged, fucking begged, watching her frantically dress and grab her keys and wallet, then fly through the door toward my office.

I dove for the towel, wrapping it around my waist as I followed her, a strangling sensation closing around my throat.

"Ava..." I called as she ran toward the front door, fumbling over the lock with clumsy fingers. But she got it open before I could even reach her and then she was out on the street, hauling ass down the sidewalk in her bare feet, her drenched hair soaking through the back of her dress.

I wanted to follow her. Fuck, I *needed* to follow her. But I couldn't go fucking chasing a soaked and freaked out woman down the street in a god damn towel. With a frustrated sigh, I went back to get dressed.

After the Session

I forced myself to calm the fuck down.

I didn't let myself chase after her.

Not right away.

I called. I texted. I left messages. I waited. I gave her space.

But when more than an hour had passed and there was nothing, I let myself get into my car and go to her place, taking up the stairs two at a time, feeling almost sick with worry.

I pounded on the door despite being told to keep my panties on by Jake. Then the door swung open, making Jake's easy grin slip immediately off of his face. It was replaced by... anger. Genuine anger.

But I didn't have time to smooth over his feelings.

"Where is she?" I demanded moving to press past the doorway.

"No," Jake said, holding onto the side of the door, blocking my way.

"I need to see her, Jake," I reasoned, running a hand through my hair, trying to calm down. She was there. She was with her people. She was alright.

"I don't think that's a good idea," Jake shook his head.

"Jake," Shay said, walking up, looking as worried as I felt. "I dunno. You haven't seen her. She's like... bad," those words fell like lead in my stomach. Bad? How bad was bad? Shay didn't exactly seem like the type to exaggerate. "Maybe it will help."

"Or it could make it worse," Jake supplied, eyeing me suspiciously. "He's the reason she flew in here soaking fucking wet and more freaked than I've ever seen her. And I've seen her freaked, Shay. He fucking did that."

"It's not what you think, Jake," I said, shaking my head.

"She needs a shrink," Shay reasoned.

"So we'll call the other one. The chick."

"Oh for fuck's sake," Shay said, obviously losing her patience. "He's here. Let him try. I'll go with him."

At this, Jake sighed, dropping his hand from the door. "Fine. But if you hurt her again, man, I'll fucking make you regret it."

"I'd expect nothing less," I nodded at him as Shay led me across the apartment to Ava's room.

I went in, but Shay stayed at the door, giving us a little bit of privacy but keeping an eye like the watchdog she was.

Ava was curled up on her bed, cheeks tear-stained, sniffling, curled up into herself.

"Baby..."

At the sound of my voice, she pulled her legs up into her chest, curling into a protective little ball and burying her face in the sleeves of her sweatshirt.

"Sweetheart," I said, reaching for her arms and pulling them away form her face. "Don't hide from me," I pleaded, but her eyes stayed downcast. "Why did you run?" I asked, not able to keep the question inside anymore.

She bit the inside of her cheek, looking completely and utterly... fucking... lost.

"You can't talk to me right now?" I asked, thinking of her mutism as I reached out to rub some stray tears from her cheeks. Her head shook as an answer and my heart broke for her a little. "Okay. That's okay," I crooned. "I want to be here for you," I said, meaning it more than I had ever meant anything. "Can I be here?" To this, I got nothing. No words. No sounds. No head shakes or nods. Nothing. "I don't feel comfortable leaving you if you can't even answer me. So I am going to stay right here, okay?" I asked, lowering myself down on the floor beside her bed. "If you need me, I'm right here. If you don't... I'm here anyway."

My hand fell from her face and as soon as it did, she curled up into herself, shutting me out. Not long later, she fell into a restless sleep.

I just sat there, going over every single second of the time in that bed, trying to figure out what I might have done or said to make her shut down on me. But in the end, I came up with nothing.

Her eyes opened slowly, eyelids painfully swollen.

"Hey," I said softly.

Then she did something completely unexpected. She reached her arms out and grabbed me, dragging me toward her. I stood up and quickly kicked out of my shoes before she could change her mind and climbed into the space beside her. "Come on," I said, stretching my arm out. "Come rest on your spot."

Before she had even moved toward me, the tears started streaming down her face again and I let my arms wrap her up gently, not wanting to freak her out any more, but needing to hold her.

"I didn't know something was wrong," I murmured, half to myself. "I would have helped you. You seemed fine. Happy even. I knew you were in there too long. I should have guessed something was up."

Silence followed, but I hadn't expected anything else. I wasn't a miracle worker. She needed time. My arms went tighter around her. "I'm proud of you for using the safe word. I know that wasn't easy for you. Especially when you were so upset. I wish you would have stayed. I wish you would have talked to me about it and not let yourself go to this place."

A minute later, Shay's shadow moved across the doorway again, pausing for a second before she came in and sat at the foot of the bed, resting her hand on Ava's leg. Letting her know she was there for her.

"Is she gonna be alright?" she asked, sounding concerned. "I've seen her panic before but this is different."

"She'll be okay," I said. She would. She had to be. No matter what. No matter how long it took, how much work it took. I broke her. I was going to fix her.

"What happened?"

I sighed. "Honestly?" I asked, shaking my head. "I don't know."

"Did you guys..."

"Yeah. But she was fine. I swear, Shay. I was paying attention." Yeah, I was trying to etch every single memory, every breath, every sigh into my soul. I didn't miss anything. "In my professional opinion, she was handling it really well."

Then Ava wasn't calm and still against me anymore. No. She shrank away. Like I disgusted her. Like she didn't want to be anywhere near me. She rolled onto her other side, facing away from me, and curling back up into her ball again.

"I guess she didn't like something you said," Shay said, standing.

"Yeah," I agreed, feeling suddenly tired. Bone deep fucking tired. Body and soul. "But fuck if I know what it was."

"Figure it out," Shay said, her tone leaving no leeway for me to screw that mission up. "I mean it, Doc. Fix her. I want her back to how she was before. She was doing so good. Going out. Being more open with me and Jake..."

"I know."

"How many more sessions are you supposed to have?"

"Four."

"What are they?" she asked bluntly.

It wasn't really right for me to tell her. At least not the specifics. But she was worried about her friend. And, well, I didn't think she was the type of woman who would back down. "More... intimacy," I hedged. "For two more sessions. Then on the ninth session, I take her out."

"For what?"

"To teach her how to handle herself around men. Flirt with them," I said, the words like venom to my system. "Shut them down if she doesn't want them. Prepare for her new life once therapy is over."

"And the last?" Shay pressed.

"Patient's choice. We can do recaps of everything. We can try a fetish if there is one she is interested in. Threesomes. Or even just... talk therapy."

"Pretty sure she ain't into threesomes."

"I know. I honestly hate those sessions anyway," I admitted, shaking my head.

"Too much work, huh?" Shay asked with a knowing smile.

"I think the only men who want them are men who have no idea what they are getting into."

"Well," Shay said, moving toward the door, "like I said... fix her. She's the best."

"I know," I said, but Shay was already gone. I was talking to myself.

I sat up for I don't know how long listening to her cry. I wanted to reach out for her. I wanted to do or say anything to help her. But she didn't want my affection and I suddenly found myself lost for words.

Finally, she fell asleep.

A while later, so did I.

I woke up alone. Again. Ava was gone. Again.

I sat up in her bed that smelled too much like her and ran my hands down my face. I was hoping that her being up was a good thing. That she wasn't just trying to get away from me again.

I got up on a sigh, moving toward the door and stopping in the doorway as I watched Ava walk out of the bathroom in jeans and a black long sleeve tee. Her wet hair was pulled back into a ponytail which only accented how swollen and red her eyes were.

"I said we both got the stomach flu from some bad take-out," Shay's voice called from the kitchen. "You 'aight?"

Ava opened her mouth to speak then turned suddenly, her eyes catching mine. Then she looked me up and down, taking in my face which likely looked as rough as I felt, then looking over my wrinkled suit.

"Ava..." I said, a thousand words caught on my tongue.

She turned to Shay for a second, who nodded, then walked toward me, waiting for me to move out of the way so we could both go in her bedroom.

I closed the door behind me as she took a deep breath as if trying to steel herself. "I'm sorry," she said, lifting her chin a little.

"Ava you have nothing to be sorry for," I said, shaking my head. "Can you tell me what happened?"

"I... had a panic attack," she said, unnecessarily. "After. Which was different and I just... didn't handle it well."

Something didn't feel right about that to me. But I couldn't place it and I couldn't press her either. "Okay. Why didn't you tell me?"

"I just... needed some space."

Again, something felt false in her words.

"Alright. I understand," I said, though I didn't because she wasn't being honest. "I wish you would have felt comfortable enough to share that with me though." Or tell me the truth right then. "So we could work it out together."

"I'll try harder next time," she said and there was a sort of determination in her words. "It just kind of snuck up on me. I was zero to ten in like two minutes."

I nodded, moving toward her, my hand rising to touch her cheek. I needed to feel connected to her again. But she shrank away, skirting past me, and going toward the door. "I think Shay is making breakfast. You're welcome to stay," she said almost robotically.

"Oh, um. I have to go home and change. I have a client at ten," I said, watching her with drawn-together brows.

"Okay. What time is our next session?" she asked in the same dead tone.

"Ava, are you sure you're alright? You seem..."

"I'm fine," she interrupted brightly, plastering on a smile that I didn't buy for a second.

I watched her for a beat, weighing whether or not to push her before deciding it wasn't the time. "Okay," I sighed. "Tomorrow at seven."

"Alright," she said as she opened the door and started leading me through the apartment. "I'll see you then. I'm sorry you needed to come out."

"I didn't *need* to come. I *wanted* to come. And it's nothing. I'll see you tomorrow," I said, not wanting to leave. I wanted, instead, to cancel all my clients and drag her back into her bedroom to force her to tell me the truth.

"Yup. See you then," she said and gave me the fake smile again and shut the door in my face.

Seventh Session

By the time seven rolled around the next night, I had calmed myself down. Thank god. Because up until then, I was ready to jump down her throat and demand a little honesty. But that was pure selfishness. So I got my shit together and got my head in the game.

The door opened and there she was in a simple long-sleeve dress.

"Ava," I said, sending her a small smile.

"Chase," she said back as she turned to lock the door.

"How are you feeling?"

"Can't complain," she shrugged, walking toward me. That was new. I was always the one to approach her.

"You sure? You seem a little..." There wasn't even a word for it. Off. Not herself. Something to that effect.

"My roommates are at each other's throats."

"Roommates?" I asked as we walked through my office and into the bedroom. "Plural?"

"Yeah, Shay is moving in," she said casually as she gave the playlist more consideration than usual. She finally hit one and then the music from a list called "fucking" came on, making me almost drop the martini I was holding out to her. "What?" she asked, feigning innocence as filthy lyrics blasted through the speakers.

"Nothing," I said, shaking my head, watching as she drained her drink.

"So session seven..." she started.

"Yeah," I said, shaking my head again. Nothing about her was right. But I gestured toward the nightstand where a basket full of sex toys was situated. "These are just here in case you want to experiment," I said, moving to stand beside her as she looked through the contents. "There is no pressure. Some of the items in there are things that some people will never have any interest in and that's fine. But I like to bring it all out because it can be easier to point out something instead of telling someone that you want to try it."

She nodded, reaching into the basket, and coming back with a lilac colored vibrator. She tossed it onto the bed with a shrug, making my cock twitch in anticipation. "Yeah?" I asked.

"Sure. Why not?" she countered, kicking out of her shoes then ripping her dress off.

I was just about to ask again what was wrong when my air hissed out of my mouth. Because she wasn't just out of her dress. She was completely fucking naked.

"You were just," I started, my voice low and deep, "walking up my street pantyless in that dress?" I asked, a smile tugging at my lips

"Yes. Now why are you still dressed?" she demanded, her voice strong.

I felt my brows draw together, my head tilting as I watched her for a minute. I wanted to ask. I really did. But if she wanted to take the lead, then there was no good reason for me to question her. Taking the lead was a big step for many women. For her, it was huge. So I was just going to enjoy it. I started taking off my clothes. She sat down on the bed, working at the plastic casing to the vibrator until she got it free.

Done undressing, I took the vibrator from her hands, twisted off the battery cap, inserted batteries, and twisted it back on.

"Lay back and spread your legs," I said, kneeling on the edge of the bed.

She immediately scooted back, letting her legs fall open. She was already wet for me. I took a steadying breath as a jolt of desire shot through my system. I brought my arm forward, running the vibrator between the folds of her pussy. She flinched away from the cold until I turned it on.

And her entire body shuddered.

Shuddered.

Hard.

Fuck me.

I moved it up toward her clit and her eyes went huge. Her mouth fell open. Her back arched. Jesus Christ. Her moans filled my ears, making the urge to get inside her overwhelm me. But I needed to see her come first. So I just kept pulsing the vibrator on her clit.

It was barely two minutes before her orgasm ripped through her violently, making her cry out and wrench away from the sensation to curl up on her side and shake through the waves.

"Jesus Christ," I groaned, turning off the vibrator and setting it aside. She was still curled into herself, her breathing erratic when I crawled onto the bed behind her, putting my hand on her hip. "Baby?"

She sucked in a breath. "I'm fine."

"You sure?" I asked her back.

"Yep. That was just... intense."

That was putting it fucking lightly.

"Yeah, I know," I said, letting my hands stroke up her spine. "Just watching you through that... fuck me."

Then suddenly, she rolled onto her back. "Go ahead," she said, making my brows draw together. Go ahead?

"What?" I asked, my hand seemingly unable to strop touching her as I stroked across her belly.

"Fuck me," she said, keeping her gaze on mine, almost like a challenge. Like she was daring me to call her on it.

"What?" I asked again, not quite believing she could be saying those words.

"I said go ahead and fuck me."

"Jesus," I hissed, shaking my head at her. Again, on a personal level, I wanted to ask her what was up. I wanted to get to the bottom of whatever was going on with her. But on a professional level, it would be stupid to try to take her power away from her.

Then she shot up off the bed, moving to the edge, making my heart fly into my chest. She wasn't going to run from me. Not again.

"Babe... what's the matter? Where are you going?"

She turned back toward me, holding out a condom foil. "Just getting something," she said, pressing it into my hand.

I broke open the condom and slipped it on, keeping my gaze on hers, trying to figure her out. But her mask was carefully in place.

God damn it.

Once the condom was on, she moved to lay down on the mattress and I grabbed her arm to stop her. "No. We did that already," I told her, watching a bit of surprise cross her face and feeling unreasonably pleased by it. At least it was a genuine reaction. "Time for something new."

"Okay," she said, shrugging.

I wanted to shake her. How the hell was I supposed to fuck her when she was being so distant? So shut down?

"Come here," I said, patting my leg.

She unfolded from herself slowly, hesitantly moving to straddle my waist. "Like this?" she asked, her tone a little shy as she rested her hand tentatively on my shoulder. Fuck yeah. There was my girl.

"Yeah, baby," I said, moving my hand between us to grab my cock and slide it down her slick cleft, making her groan, making her bite into her lip. "You're going to ride me. Show me how you like being fucked."

Her eyes went wide for a second before getting heavy with desire. "Okay."

As soon as I heard the word, I pressed my cock against the threshold to her pussy, waiting. "You're in control," I reminded her and a small smile toyed with her lips. She took a deep breath and started to press her body down into mine. Her tight pussy grabbed at me as I spread her slowly, inch by inch. "That's it, baby. Take me in."

Then she did. Deep. To the hilt, feeling my cock hit at an angle it hadn't the last time, stroking over a spot that made her forehead fall down to my shoulder on a primal groan.

"You're so fucking tight," I told her, my hands digging into her ass. "You feel how your pussy is squeezing me?" Against my shoulder, she nodded. I pressed my hips up into hers slightly. "Find what feels good, Ava," I told her, my hands moving to her hips.

She lifted her head as she shifted upward, moving until I was half out of her before pressing all the way back in, moaning.

"That feel good?"

Her pussy tightened around me. "Yeah," she whimpered, lifting up again.

She pushed back down. "Try this, baby," I said, taking her hips and moving them back then forward, letting my cock rub hard against her g-spot.

"Oh my god," she cried, her fingers digging into my shoulder.

Fuck. The sound of her when my cock was inside her... it was almost my undoing. It took everything I had to hold myself off. "Make yourself come, Ava."

It didn't take long. Her g-spot proved every bit as sensitive as her clit as she rocked against me. It came on slow, a hard tightening around me followed by a slow, deep pulsating as she collapsed against me, gasping, her nails drawing blood from my shoulders.

I stroked my hands up and down her spine, giving her a minute to recover, but knowing I was nowhere near finished with her.

She moved backward, her brows drawing together when she felt me still hard inside her.

I felt the smile toy at my lips. "Yeah, I'm not done with you yet," I told her and her pussy clenched hard, making the smile spread. "You like that idea, don't you?"

She fought a smile and pursed her lips. "Eh, maybe," she said, feigning indifference but the vice grip of her cunt on me told a whole other story.

I chuckled, taking her by the hips and tossing her onto the mattress. "All fours," I said, my voice stern, unable to keep the edge out of my tone. She rolled onto her belly but didn't rise up as I moved to stand at the edge of the bed. Too far gone to give a fuck about reining in my natural dominant tendencies, I grabbed her ankles and dragged her toward me until her knees were at the edge. "I said all fours," I growled. There wasn't even a pause as she got up on all fours. "Good girl," I said, my hands squeezing her ass. My palms moved down the backs of her thighs, just to the spot where they met high up to hide her pussy and I slapped that spot hard. "Now spread your legs."

She spread her legs.

"I am going to fuck you," I told her, sliding my cock to her pussy and holding there. My hand moved up her back toward her neck then into her hair, grabbing it and pulling until her body jerked up toward me. "Hard," I added as I slammed inside her. Her breath hissed out of her and her ass arched higher. "Elbows on the bed," I told her and she moved down, making me pull her hair even harder. But she didn't pull away.

She liked it. Maybe even as much as I did. My other hand moved to right above her ass.

Then I fucked her.

Hard.

Like I fucking promised.

And she fucking loved it.

Each time, I withdrew almost all the way before slamming fully back in, tilting up slightly. Wild. Primal.

My hand twisted harder in her hair as my other hand moved to her hip and used it to pull her back against me with each forward thrust, getting as deep as possible.

She was clutching the sheets, burying her face in them as she screamed. Not moaned. Not groaned. Not cried out. *Screamed.*

"I want to *hear* you come," I scolded, yanking her up by her hair.

I slammed forward and she came.

And the entire *block* could hear her.

"Fuck fuck fuck fuck," she cried as the pulsations kept ripping through her and I slammed the whole way through it. "Chase..."

That was it.

I was done.

I thrust forward, burying deep, and came hard enough to see white.

"Fucking perfect," I groaned, letting go of her hair and she collapsed forward onto the bed.

I waited until my legs felt less wobbly and made my way to the bathroom to deal with the condom before I went back to the bed, settling onto my back and staring at the ceiling. "Come here," I said, patting my chest.

But she didn't move.

She just stayed on her belly, making some weird grumbling sound in her throat that made me chuckle. "A little come-drunk, huh?"

"Shut up," she grumbled, her words heavy, sleepy.

I laughed, shaking my head at her, letting my hand land on her ass and squeeze it.

"That was fucking amazing," I told her. Meaning it.

She made another noise that sounded like agreement.

I smiled down at her as I shifted to start planting kisses from the base of her neck downward. Suddenly, her body wasn't numb and lifeless anymore. I felt her arch into the feel of my lips on her spine, over her ass, down her thigh to her ankle, and then up the other leg. I wanted to know every single inch of her. I wanted to commit the feel and taste of her skin to memory. I kissed back up her spine and across her shoulder before moving away to lie back down again.

Then she was moving and I felt a swelling in my chest, knowing she was coming to me. She was going to rest her head on my chest and all would feel right in the world.

But then she got up on all fours then landed her ass back onto her ankles, too far out of reach. Something was wrong. The swelling in my chest deflated, leaving me feeling hollow.

"Wait... where are you going?" I asked as she inched away.

"I promised Shay I would help her set up her room tonight," she lied. *Lied.* To my face.

What the fuck was going on?

"Ava..."

But then she was off the bed and dragging her dress over her head.

She was going to leave me. And I had no way to make her stay.

So I moved off the bed to grab my pants.

"What are you doing?" she asked.

"I'm walking you to your car," I said, standing and reaching for my shirt as I slipped into my shoes. "You're not walking around at night with no fucking panties on," I told her, my words taking an edge toward cold.

144

She rolled her eyes. *Rolled her fucking eyes* as she reached for her keys and wallet and made her way out of the office.

I fell into step beside her as we walked in stony silence.

She got to her car, unlocked the door, and threw her shit on the passenger seat before turning to face me.

I . Couldn't. Fucking. Take. It. Anymore.

I grabbed her, pushing her back against her car.

"Chase... what the hell..."

"What is wrong with you?" I demanded, getting close.

Her eyes went wide, guilty, before she pushed it away. "Nothing," she said, scrunching up her face like I was the one being crazy.

"Bullshit. You've been off since you woke up the other morning and kept giving me that fake ass smile. What is going on with you?"

She took a deep breath. "Nothing is wrong with me. I've been... *learning* a lot."

"What the fuck..." I started to explode before reining it in, taking a deep breath. "You're not being you," I said more calmly. Even to my own ears, my words sounded sad.

"You've only seen me for a couple hours here and there, Chase. You have no idea who I really am."

"I know you," I countered, feeling my jaw getting tight. "I fucking *know* you. This," I said viciously, "is not you." I paused, watching her blank face. "Fuck it," I said and lowered my lips to hers.

It should have been hard and rough and bruising with the blood boiling inside me. But the second our bodies touched, my lips gentled. It was soft. Teasing. *Loving.* Her lips fell open on a whimper and my tongue stroked inside to toy with hers. Easy. Lazy. And then I pulled away slowly, my hand stroking down her cheek.

Her eyes fluttered open and I felt my face soften at the look I found there.

"There. That's my Ava."

Her eyes went panicked for a second before she expertly slipped the mask back on.

"And she's gone," I said, not even fucking caring how disappointed my voice sounded.

"So sorry to disappoint you," she said, her tone icy. Icy. Ava wasn't cold. Ava was sweet and warm and as close to perfect as I had ever seen. Something was wrong. And she didn't want to share it with me.

I closed my eyes and took a breath, trying to slip back into professional mode. It was the only way to save myself. "Tomorrow. Seven."

"Fine," she snapped, wrenching away from me and dropping into her seat. "I'll see you tomorrow."

Then the door slammed.

And fake Ava was gone.

And she took *my* fucking Ava with her.

After the Session

I sat in my office the next day, my afternoon cleared of patients, trying to keep my mind off of Ava. I tried to keep my mind off of the fact that we just had three more sessions. I tried to keep my mind off the idea that I might never even peek at my Ava again before I would stop seeing the fake one again. For good.

"Chase," Mary, my receptionist's voice called, making me start. She sent me a guilty smile. "I knocked first," she explained, standing in the doorway.

I waved a hand. "Sorry. I was somewhere else," I admitted, sitting back.

"You have a call," she explained, gesturing toward the phone on my desk.

"Who is it?" I asked, sounding every bit as tired as I felt.

"Mae," she said with a fondness in her tone. Mae called every week like clockwork. When I was with a patient, she would chat with Mary.

"Oh, right," I said, feeling a heaviness in my chest. I loved Mae, but talking to Mae would only mean more disappointment. Because despite knowing her for the better part of a decade, despite being the only one she talked to about what happened to her and her worries and fears and anxieties, I had never been able to help.

Mae was in her early thirties and the only time she had sex was when she was a freshmen in college. Non-consenting sex. She never let another man come within a foot of her again.

She was doing well. She had a gorgeous house and a thriving career in an energy company. She had friends (female). She had a slew of hobbies that kept her busy.

"I'm satisfied," she told me one afternoon a few months before.

"Satisfied isn't happy, Mae. It isn't fulfilled."

"Says the man who has a different woman every other day," she teased. "How fulfilling can that be?"

And, well, she had a point.

Casual sex was good. At times, it was great. Fulfilling in a very physical, very hollow kind of way. But she was right. It wasn't emotionally or even mentally fulfilling. It didn't bring with it real happiness.

At the time, though, I had no idea what a bitter kind of misery came along with real happiness.

A part of me wondered if I was better off never knowing it in the first place.

"You're never going to stop trying to fix me, huh?" she laughed.

"You're not broken," I insisted. "But, no, I'm never going to stop trying to help you."

I hung up an hour later, feeling both pleased and forlorn. She was doing well. But there was no end in sight to her resistance. Maybe it was time to stop trying to help her. She said she was content. Who the hell was I to question that?

Especially given that I didn't know what the fuck was going on in my own life. I was in no place to judge her.

I fell in love with a fucking patient for chrissakes.

I got into my car and started driving toward the Italian place I took Ava, a creature of habit always. But I stopped halfway there, remembering Ava insisting the small place by her apartment was the best she had ever had. And, before even making the decision logically, I turned around and headed in that direction.

Maybe a part of me was angry with her. But a bigger, more prominent part just wanted to know her better. Know the things she liked. The places she frequented.

"For fuck's sake," I said to myself, shaking my head. I was starting to sound like a fucking stalker. But I parked and went into the beat up Italian place around the corner from her place.

The black and white checkered floors were worn but the bright red paint on the walls was fresh. The counter and tables were made of an old, beat-up wood that was soft with age. The bell chimed as I walked in and a man came out of the back, his belly spilling over his waistband, a thick mustache over a severe mouth. "Eat," he said, pushing a menu toward me.

I nodded was I went over to a table to sit and look over my options.

I had just ordered when the bell over the door chimed and my head snapped up automatically.

It was like a kick to the gut. Or a fall from a swing. It was like the wind was knocked out of me.

Because there she was- looking fresh and relaxed, smiling at the owner who barked the same word he barked at me, at her. "Yes," she said and held up her hand, showing him three fingers and he shuffled off.

I don't know what came over me then, but it was something dark and bitter that made my words come out almost cruel, "Hey there, *stranger*..."

149

She jumped, spinning to face me. Her eyes went huge as she stared. "What are you doing here?"

"A girl I know told me this is the best Italian. I came to see for myself."

It happened fast. Fast enough that she went from a one to a ten in a blink. Her eyes got huge, her hand moved to her throat like she was suffocating.

The dark and bitter was washed away among a wave of bone-deep concern. "Ava... hey," I started, my voice calm and soothing. "Take a breath."

But a few seconds passed and she didn't, her eyes getting bigger and bigger, her body starting to shake slightly.

Then she turned and ran.

By the time I got up and to the door to follow her, she was lost in the crowd.

"Fuck!" I yelled loud enough for the owner to come out of the back, brows drawn down. Seeing me, he just shrugged and disappeared again.

When he came back out with a huge bag and looked around, saying, "Trè?", I just raised my hand and pulled out my wallet. If she went anywhere, she went home. So I paid, took the bag, and I walked toward her apartment building.

"Hey, Dr. Sexy," Shay greeted with a smile, but a brow was lifted.

"She here?" I asked, pushing past her.

"No man," Jake said from the kitchen. "She ran to get Italian."

"Here's your Italian," I said, shoving the bag toward his chest.

"Chase, what's going on?" Shay asked, tone firm.

"I was at the Italian place and Ava came in. She had a panic attack and flew out of there before I could calm her down." Jake and Shay shared a look. A pointed one. It was a look that said a thousand words. They knew something. They knew something that I wasn't going to be let in on. "What's going on guys?"

150

Shay opened her mouth to speak, but Jake cut her off. "Dunno man. She just has those things sometimes."

The door opened half an hour later and in walked Ava, looking calmer. She wasn't completely back to normal, but she was alright. She was at a five. Not great, but getting better.

"Well, finally," Jake greeted her, his mouth full since he ripped open the bags ten minutes before declaring 'it's not like it's going to help her anxiety for us to go hungry'. "Just leave us here to fucking starve. Luckily Chase here cared enough about our..."

Ava's eyes fell to me and everything else became background noise.

"Are you okay?"

She took a deep breath and I braced for the mask to fall into place. But it didn't. "Better," she said, placing her purse down on the table beside the door and moving across the apartment.

"Yo, where did ya' go?" Shay asked, making both of us turn our heads in her direction.

My gaze quickly turned back to Ava. "I had a phone session with Dr. Bowler."

My stomach twisted to the point of genuine pain. She had a session with Dr. Bowler. She had gone out of her way to contact her other shrink, probably calling her away from other patients, to talk to her. I had been right there. I had been *right there* and she didn't turn to me.

"Ava... why didn't you talk to me?"

She shook her head, unable to meet my gaze. "I don't know. I just... panicked. I needed to get out of that place. Once I got somewhere, I picked up my phone and..."

"You could have called *me*," I said quietly, closing the space between us.

"I just... wasn't thinking," she said, looking up at me from under my lashes. The vulnerability in her eyes made me want to wrap her up so nothing could ever make her feel that way again. But that wasn't my fucking place.

"It's okay," I said, allowing my hand to move out and stroke her cheek. "As long as you're alright."

"I am. That was just... a bad one."

"Okay," I said, my hand trailing from her cheek to her neck, then resting on her shoulder. Ava's gaze slid past me to where Shay and Jake were, no doubt, watching us intensely. I made my hand drop on a slow exhale. "I'll see you in forty minutes, okay? Or I can wait here if you're still not feeling well."

"I'm okay," she said, looking me in the eye. "I'm just going to shower and change and I'll be over."

I made my voice drop so that only she could hear me, leaning in slightly. "Okay, baby. I'll be waiting for you."

I let her open the door and close it behind me, sinking back against it for a moment, looking for the strength to keep going.

It took longer than my pride would let me admit.

But eventually, I left.

I went to my office and I waited to see which version of her I would get that night.

Eighth Session

I had been prepared for a lot of things. Or, at least, that was what I was tried to tell myself. No matter what Ava I was faced with, I was going to handle it. Calmly. With at least a semblance of professionalism.

But that was before I walked out of my office to find Ava already inside the front door.

"Ava..."

Then her hand went to the button of her coat, pushed it through the hole, and discarded the material. *That dress.* Red material in the shape of an hourglass in the front, the sides and straps made of a see through black mesh-like material. It clung like a second skin and... that *body* in that *dress*...

"*Fuck me,*" I growled. Then she lifted her chin and moved in a slow circle, showing me the back which was the same see through black mesh from the straps to *very* low on her hips. I held an arm out, wanting her to come toward me. She did. As soon as she was close enough, I slid my hands down her arms and took her hands. "You are *so* fucking beautiful."

She swallowed hard before speaking. "Thank you."

My hands squeezed hers and led them to my shoulders. One of my hands went to her lower back, pressing her body to mine as my other moved to her jaw, tilting her face toward mine. "There she is," I said, half to myself. "I missed her." And I fucking did.

I lowered my face to hers, sinking in deep. I kissed her like it was the first time. Like it was the last. She kissed me back like her soul recognized the need in mine. Her body pressed into mine. Her hands went around my neck.

"Okay," I said, pulling away. "Bed. Now."

I grabbed her hand, holding it tight, as I led her through the office, past the sidebar and toward the bed. I sat, pulling her upright body between my open legs, and looked up at her. I felt my heart in my eyes and I didn't even fucking try to mask it.

"Do you want to know about this session?" I asked, beginning to loathe the formality of it all.

Her hand moved out, brushing a strand of my hair back off my forehead, her fingers trailing down the side of my face and my neck until her palm flattened on my shoulder. "Sure."

"This all depends on your limits, okay? Just because this is the way it is planned out, doesn't mean it is the way it has to be. If you're not into it, we move onto something else. Okay?"

Her brows furrowed a little. "Okay."

Right to the chase, I asked, "How do you feel about anal sex?" I watched, looking for any sign of anxiety, especially given her panic attack earlier.

Anal sex was a touchy subject. Always. Professionally. Personally. Most men wanted it but were afraid to ask about it. Many women were curious but too afraid to admit it. So even extremely experienced, sexually confident women had gone without it when they harbored a secret desire for it. Which made asking Ava about it incredibly nerve-wrecking.

"Ava..." I said when a long silence hung between us.

"I'm thinking," she said, rolling her eyes at me.

"Alright," I said, my hands sliding down her thighs to push up her skirt a little so she could straddle me. "Then why don't you come here and think about it?" I suggested.

She didn't hesitate, just climbed up on my lap and rested her head against my shoulder. The sweetness of it made the days full of frustration and confusion slip away. My arms went around her, holding her close.

"It's okay if you're not into it."

"I don't know if I am into it or not."

"That's alright," I said, my hands sliding up and down her back, the feel of her body heat through the silky mesh material was positively erotic. "Do you think you want to try it?" I asked, attempting to keep hopefulness out of my voice.

There was a pause before her sweet lips pressed into my neck. "Yes."

I closed my eyes, taking a deep breath. "Good girl," I said, turning my face slightly so I could kiss the side of her head. "We'll start with regular sex first though, okay? Get you all warmed up."

"Okay."

"Okay. Now get a condom," I said, slapping her ass playfully, trying to put her at ease. She laughed, hopping off of me and coming back with a condom that I took and laid on the bed beside me. "Arms up," I instructed and then ever so slowly inched the material off of her body, enjoying watching her skin flush in desire. Material gone, she moved to step out of her shoes. "No," I said, a little too firm. "The shoes stay on."

I let my eyes rake over her body from her black red-bottom fuck-me heels to her soft hair, then back over it all again. Until she was squirming under my gaze. Slowly, shockingly, she lowered herself down on her knees before me. Her hands moved out toward my belt, unfastening it and then pulled my zipper open. I watched, already hard as fucking steel, as she reached inside and pulled out my cock. She leaned forward and quickly sucked me down to the hilt, making my hand slam down on the crown of her head.

"Fuck, baby. So sweet," I murmured and she started to suck me. Slow. Soft. Flicking her tongue over the head at every pass. I let myself sink into the sensation for a long time until I felt the clawing need for release get closer. "Okay. *Fuck.* Okay. Baby, stop," I said and she moved away, sitting back on her heels and smiling at me. Proud. She was proud of herself. And happy.

Jesus Christ.

I wanted to see her looking just like that forever.

But that wasn't in my stars.

"Panties off. On the bed," I instructed and watched as she shimmied out of her thong and crawled into the bed beside me, lying down. I stood, watching her as I removed my clothes. "Legs straight up," I told her. Up they went. "Cross your ankles." She crossed her ankles, giving me a view of her perfect legs, her sweet little ass, and her pussy. "Fuck, fuck me," I groaned, tossing aside my shirt. "This view, baby? Fucking perfect."

I reached for the condom, slipping it on, then moved a finger up her slick folds, finding her clit and circling it. She whimpered, her legs moving downward. "I said legs up, ankles crossed."

Her legs went up again and I moved closer, taking her ankles and placing them against one of my shoulders. In one thrust, I was buried deep in her pussy.

"Ohmygod," she groaned, her thighs and pussy clenching.

"You can hold me as tight as you want like this, can't you baby?" I asked, kissing the side of her ankle. As if testing my theory, she tightened more. And I couldn't hold off anymore. But it wasn't hard. It was just fast. My cock buried deep and my hips slammed into her thighs over and over so that I needed to wrap my arms around her knees to hold her body still as I fucked her.

I felt the vice grip of her pre-orgasm and quickly pulled away before it was too late.

"No!" she cried, reaching for me.

"Up on the bed, baby. All fours," I said softly, letting her legs fall.

She moved onto all fours and I pressed her legs wider with my knees as I reached for the vibrator.

"It doesn't always feel good right away," I said, stroking her soft ass. "If it hurts, tell me. I don't want to hurt you." I leaned down and kissed one of her ass cheeks gently. The last thing in the world I wanted to do was hurt her. "I'll be gentle until you tell me otherwise."

"Okay," she said as I slid my cock into place, pressing but not pushing forward. I reached for the vibrator, turned it on, but didn't put it to her clit. "Just breathe, babe," I reminded her as I started pushing forward slowly. Her body tensed, jerked. "Ava, breathe," I said, moving the vibrator to her clit. Her legs shook with the sensation. "Is it too much?" I asked, hoping to god it wasn't. "I just have the head in. If it hurts too much..."

"It's okay," she said, breathing deep.

I steeled my resolve to go slow and kept inching my way in. She flinched every inch or so and I paused to let her adjust. Her ass arched up for better access as I pressed fully in. She reached for the vibrator, taking it from my hands and turning it off. "You okay?"

"Yeah?" she half-asked, half-declared.

"Does it hurt?"

"No."

Thank fuck.

"Does it feel good?" she didn't answer for a moment. "Baby?"

"Yes," she admitted a little timidly.

A growl type rumbling came through my chest. "I want it to feel good," I told her, rocking my hips into her. It was barely a movement at all, just a pulsing. My hands went around her and up her belly to cup her breasts. I pressed into her chest, pulling her backward until her back was resting against my chest. One of my arms went around her hips, the other around her chest above her breasts, holding her far too tightly against me but she didn't complain and I didn't want to let go.

My hips started dropping then moving back upward into her. Over and over. Until her breathing started to hitch. "Tell me it feels good." I needed to hear it.

"It feels good," she said on a groan.

"No one has ever been in here before, have they?"

"No."

"It's all mine," I said, sliding in again, claiming it.

"It's all yours," she agreed breathlessly.

Fuck me.

I kept the slow, steady rocking, enjoying the sweetness of it. It wasn't sex. It wasn't fucking. It was lovemaking. And I felt completely lost in it.

"Chase?"

"Yeah, baby?"

"Harder," she said, her hands moving to my forearm and digging in.

I didn't need more encouragement than that. I gave it to her. Happily. I jerked up into her. Faster. Harder. Like she wanted it.

"Chase?" she asked a few minutes later, sounding like she needed assurance.

"You're going to come for me, baby, and I don't even need to touch your pussy. You can come for me just like this and I will feel it."

That was what she needed to hear. To let go.

She came hard, her entire body jerking as she pulsated hard. "Fuck, baby. Yeah. Just like that," I said in her ear. "I can feel you coming." And I could feel myself get there too. "Fuck. *Ava...*"

I held her after. Just as tight as before. I never wanted to fucking let go. I kissed a trail up the side of her face, resting against her temple. Her arms went upward, wrapping around my neck. "So sweet," I murmured, leaning over to kiss her arm before I untangled them from me and moved away from her.

She scrambled onto the bed and under the covers and I felt a rush of relief that she wasn't running out on me again. When I came back from the bathroom, she was curled up on her side facing the wall and I crawled in behind her, pulling her body into mine as I wrapped into her. I took her hand and squeezed. "Are you okay?"

"Yeah."

"That was..." Fuck. There were no words that came close. "Spectacular," I decided, still feeling that it was lacking.

She wiggled back into me and I pulled her tighter. Slowly but surely, her body got more and more stiff. "What are you thinking about? You're tense," I told her, nuzzling into her neck. "Talk to me."

"I was wondering about the next session," she said and it was my turn to get tense. The next session. The next session where I was going to take her out and teach her how to flirt with other men. Other men that she might eventually go home with. Men who would hold her like I was holding her. Claim her like I had claimed her. The only difference would be that they had that right... *and I didn't.* "Chase?" she asked, snuggling back into me and it was then that I saw that I had put so much space between us that we were barely even touching anymore.

"Tomorrow is Friday."

"Yeah..."

"Tomorrow I will take you out to a bar or club," I started, my words robotic. "You will dress for it. Whoever helped you with the dress tonight, if anyone, that's what you need to wear." For other men to look at.

"I can do that."

"You'll meet me here and we will drive to the destination together. You can have a drink or two, but no more than that." I, however, was going to need a fucking fifth of scotch to get through the night. "And then you will do what I tell you to approach men, or what to say when they approach you."

"And where will you be?"

"There," I said, pulling away from her again. "Watching." I was barely holding her. I couldn't. If I held her, I would feel the enormity of what I was losing.

"So the purpose is..."

"To get you comfortable interacting with other men, not just me. But having me there to be a support system if you need it." Fuck. Support her. While other men got the privilege of getting to know her. "We will go in together, sit down, and discuss how to go about... flirting," I forced the word out and it felt slimy on my tongue. "After you get comfortable doing so with me, I will excuse myself to the bar. Then you will go to the other end of the bar."

"By myself?"

"Yes. By yourself. Men get intimated by women with their female friends and won't approach a woman there with a man."

"Okay."

"Then when a man comes up to you..."

"If," she said, shaking her head.

She had no idea, no fucking idea what a prize she was. Or how unworthy we all were to try to win her.

"When," I corrected her more firmly, "a man comes up to you..."

"What?" she broke in. "Is this some positive thinking nonsense? If I believe in it enough, suddenly hoards of men will come flocking to me?"

I sighed, moving further away so I could push her onto her back and look down at her.

"How is it possible that you don't see how gorgeous you are?"

"Chase... really... I'm not..."

No. Nope. I wasn't going to listen to her talk herself down again.

"Shut up," I said, shaking my head. "Don't you dare finish that sentence." My hand moved to the side of her face, cradling her jaw. "How many times have I told you how beautiful you are? And you still don't believe me."

"It's not that. It's..."

"It's what?"

"It's... twenty-some odd years of not feeling that way. Of no one saying that to me. It's not like I am going to transform my thinking overnight. But I'm getting better. I mean... could you picture the me who walked in here for my introductory session wearing the dress I wore tonight?"

She had me there. "That's a good point. Do you believe me when I say you're beautiful?" I asked and the look came back. The look I hoped was gone for good. "There," I said, grabbing her face a little hard. "That look. What is that look? You've been giving it to me a lot lately."

"What look?" she asked, but there had been a guilty pause.

I let go of her face, rolled onto my back, and raked a hand down my face. "You're killing me, woman."

"I'll go," she said, already moving to the far end of the bed.

"That's not what I meant," I said, trying to reach for her, but she was too far and too determined to move away.

"I know," she said in a small voice. "But it's late."

"Baby..." I said, my voice a distinct plea.

She paused, grabbing her dress, and turning to me. "Yeah?"

There was so much to say: I want you. Don't leave. Don't leave me here like this, with my heart in my hands. Not one moment of this has been therapy for me. I fucking love you. I want to stop this facade. I want you to know the truth...

But none of it could be said.

161

"I'll see you tomorrow," she said once she slipped into her dress and tentatively touched my foot for the barest of seconds.

"Seven," I agreed, watching her move to grab her keys and wallet.

"As usual," she said, going out into my office.

I didn't follow. I couldn't.

I just had to let her go.

I needed the practice.

For when I needed to do it for good.

After the Session

My mother got me back briefly when I was twelve. It was my third time being pulled out of the system and put back in her care. She pee tested clean for six months. She went to her weekly meetings. She got a place that wasn't crawling with roaches. In the system's eyes, she was fit again.

Unfortunately, the system didn't know that her problem wasn't the booze or the drugs. Her problem was her own head. Her problem was she was severely bipolar. They just so happened to catch her on the mania side. The side where she was full of life and energy. The side where she was hyper goal-oriented and able to speak rapidly and never ending-ly about her plans for the future.

They saw the good mom. They saw a woman trying to get her life back on track. They saw someone determined and excited.

What they didn't see was the sleeplessness. They didn't see that she could go three days without nodding off once. They didn't see that her judgment was off and her goals and plans became more and more grandiose and unattainable.

Then they didn't see as the mania gave way to the depressive side a short six weeks later. They didn't see her curled up under her covers on her bed for weeks at a time, crying, telling me how hopeless it all was. They didn't listen as she would sit up late at night talking about horrifying, morbid stories she had read about suicide. About how jumpers finally felt free of stress because their fate was decided, there was no going back. How cutters could feel a surge of indescribable euphoria when they sliced into their skin with a razor.

Then they definitely didn't see when she started having her drug dealer come to the apartment. They didn't see her sitting at the dining room table while he tied her off and loaded up the needle. They didn't see the needle slide into the bruised crook of her elbow or watch as her head rolled back as she stared at the ceiling while the heroin worked its way into her system.

I got those constant ups and downs for a year. Because I was older. Smarter. I washed my own clothes so I didn't go to school dirty. I had perfect attendance. I got good grades. I did everything right. There was no cause for concern.

That was until I got home after soccer practice one night and found my mom at the dining room table (nothing new), her arm tied off and a needle in her elbow (normal sight), her head titled up to the ceiling with unseeing eyes (again, typical).

The differences came on me slowly. Her dealer wasn't there. He always hung around afterward. I didn't know (and frankly didn't want to) if it was the euphoria from the drugs that made them want to do it or if was the way my mother paid for the drugs in the first place, but they always screwed when they got high.

Him being gone was not normal.

Neither was the fact that she hadn't turned to greet me with pinned eyes.

Neither was the fact that her chest wasn't rising and falling.

My backpack hit the ground with a loud thud as I ran over to her, instinctively reaching my hand toward her neck to feel for a pulse. But my palm found cold skin.

She was dead.

She was dead and I was going back into the system.

And there was nothing I could do about it.

The feeling of hopelessness I felt in that moment was akin to how I felt as I sat in my office after hours on a Friday night waiting for Ava to arrive. Knowing that when she did arrive, I would be taking her out and teaching her how to invite other men into her life. Men who weren't me. Men who might treat her badly. Men who wouldn't understand her limitations. Or, somehow worse yet, men who would. Men who would give her everything she needed. Men who would take the memory of me and blur it completely until I might as well never have existed for her.

And there was nothing I could do about it.

Ninth Session

Seven rolled around and she wasn't in my office. Ava was compulsively on time or early. I felt nerves seep into my system, making my skin feel foreign and electric. What if she didn't show? What if she thought she had learned enough? What if that cold dismissal from the night before was the last I would see or hear from her? What if...

The door swung open and in she walked.

"You're late," I observed.

"Yeah," she said, completely unapologetic. She turned to lock the door, then remembered the plan for the night and stopped.

"Good for you," I said, smirking, nodding my head at her. I was proud that she didn't rush to say she was sorry. "Let's see that dress, baby."

She took off her jacket.

Head to toe- she was screaming 'take me!'

First, there was the dress. It was less of a dress and more of a bra and ridiculously short mini skirt connected with more of that see through black-mesh stuff that dresses seemed to be made with more and more often. Her hair was straightened. Someone went at her eye makeup with a heavy hand, making her brown eyes pop. She had on semi-opaque stockings that highlighted her shapely legs and led down to black heels that criss-crossed over the tops of her feet.

Jesus Christ.

In any other situation, I would have loved it. I would have taken pride in having a woman looking like she looked, dressed how she was dressed hanging off my arm.

But she wasn't dressed like that for me.

She was dressed like that for other men.

"Is this too much?" she asked self-consciously as I stared at her. "Shay told me it would work for like... all the bars and clubs, but I am seriously starting to question her fashion sense."

I felt my lips quirk up. She was still my Ava. Even if she looked like a sex kitten. "It's a nice dress," I said as I moved toward her, "but it looks extraordinary on *you*," I clarified as my hand rose to skim across the mesh covering her belly. I took a deep breath, expecting to inhale the sweet vanilla scent that always clung to her, a scent that matched her perfectly. Instead, it was something else. Sharper. Stronger. "You don't smell like you," I said and it came out like an accusation.

"Shay's perfume."

"Your eyes," I said, holding in a sigh. It was all just... too fucking much. She didn't need it. She was her own brand of simple, understated beauty without all the adornments.

"Fake eyelashes," she explained. "Apparently they make my eyes pop or something."

"They popped just fine on their own," I told her, my hand moving to stroke her cheek.

She took a slow, shaky breath. "Should I take them off?" she asked, the vulnerability clear in her tone.

167

"No," I said, shaking my head and dropping my hand. "They're fine. Most guys will appreciate the effort." Guys who didn't realize she was perfect bare-faced in jeans and a tee.

"So, um," she mumbled, looking down at her own feet. The insecurity started to hum around her like an aura. "Where are we going?"

"You're nervous," I observed as her gaze stayed downcast.

"Yeah."

"Why?"

"I've never been good with the whole... flirting thing."

I took a breath, feeling my jaw get tense. "That's what I'm here for. To teach you." I paused and when my mouth opened again, I said something I hadn't been planning to, something that was just a pathetic attempt to delay the inevitable, "We're going to start at a restaurant. Get some food in your stomach to help with the anxiety..." Her eyes flew up to mine, her brows drawn together. "I'm assuming you have, once again, not eaten before coming here."

"No," she admitted with a shrug.

"Alright," I said, reaching to open the door behind her. "Let's go. It's getting late."

I clenched my hands into fists at my side, forcing myself to not touch her. In fact, I kept a good foot between us at all time. If I touched her, it would only make things worse.

So we got in the car and I drove to A Restaurant, parking out front. I opened her door but didn't help her out even though I felt her eyes boring into me. When she climbed out, the sound of her genuine laughter made my face turn to her to find her bent half forward as she looked at the hellhole I had brought her to.

"Seriously?" she asked, still laughing, the sound making a warm sensation sweep through my body.

And just like that, my shields fell.

"Don't judge it by how it looks," I said, letting my hand land on her hip.

"So what does A Restaurant serve?" she asked as I led her inside. I let out a small laugh that had her turning her head to look at me, brows drawn together. "I don't trust that laugh," she told me as I reached for two menus after being told to 'plant ourselves anywhere'.

I led her to a table and handed her a menu, smiling to myself.

"Really?" she asked, looking up with a big smile after reading that her choices were: chicken, cow, pig, or green stuff. "So is food poisoning a part of the plan or just an added benefit?"

I opened my mouth to answer when the waitress walked over and barked, "What do you want?"

Ava looked at me, shaking her head and I ordered us each chicken.

"Truly a charming little establishment," Ava said as the waitress walked away.

"You'll understand when you try the food. So Ava," I said, making my tone slip into the professional curiosity that belonged to a therapist, "when was the last time you had a date?"

A darkness came over her features but she shrugged. "Over a year ago. Probably closer to two."

"How did that go? Where did you meet? Was it just one date?"

"Online dating site," she said with a blush. "We went to dinner. It was... forced and... awkward."

"And? I pressed.

"And we went back to his place," she said, her voice small as her pointer finger started rubbing along a dent on the wooden tabletop.

She didn't want to talk about it. It wasn't a good memory. Which was all the more reason she needed to talk about it.

"Even though it was forced and awkward?"

"Yeah." More rubbing.

169

"Why?"

She shrugged a little. "I figured I would give it another shot."

I fought the urge to reach across the table, take that hand that she was worrying against the table, and wrap it in mine.

"It didn't go well."

Her face fell even further. "No."

"Ava..." I started in a tone that was demanding more than what she was telling me. She picked up on it and stiffened. But then the food was dropped noisily on the table, effectively cutting off the conversation.

"No more online dating," I told her.

"What? Why not?"

"Because it's too easy for you. You get to hide behind your computer screen and find the match who is the least threatening. You'll slip right back into your shell. You need to... get out and experience things, Ava."

"Well," she said, shifting uncomfortably, "I am experiencing the best chicken I've ever had in my life," she said, trying to end the conversation.

"Ava..."

"I don't want a lecture, Chase," she snapped, making my brow raise at her tone.

"I wasn't..."

"Yes," she said, her tone firm, "you were. And you were being a condescending ass about it too."

Damn.

She was right.

But also... damn she was fucking sexy as hell when she was riled.

"Good for you," I said, nodding at her.

"Good for me, what?"

"Standing up for yourself," I said, smiling. "Even if you're wrong."

"I'm not wrong," she countered, getting more and more annoyed. "I don't know what is up with you tonight, but you're kind of being a jerk and it's annoying."

"Annoying?" I asked, close to laughing.

"Yes. Annoying. And frustrating," she said, nodding for emphasis. "Why are you smiling?" she asked, her eyes lowered at me.

"A couple weeks ago," I started, "do you think you would have been able to call me an ass, a jerk, annoying, and frustrating... to my face?"

Realization hit her face. "Probably not."

"Definitely not."

"So... what?" she asked, sounding riled again. "This was some kind of a test?"

"Not really, no," I said, not able to admit to her what it really was- me trying to protect myself.

"So you're just in a foul mood for no good reason?"

I watched her for a minute, the urge to tell her so strong that I didn't trust myself to speak until I got myself under control.

"I have a good reason, but it is inconsequential. Anyway," I said, pushing my plate away. I needed to steer the conversation into safer territory. "We are going to Chaos from here."

I watched as that information settled. She pushed her plate away and reached for her water. "I'm ready when you are," she said in a way that suggested that was as far from the truth as possible.

I nodded though, throwing down money and leading her back out to the car. We both wanted to get the god-forsaken night over with.

We walked up to Chaos ten minutes later, bypassing the line because I was on the list. I led her inside and into the VIP lounge, knowing she was nowhere near ready for the swarm that was the downstairs common area. She probably had her heart in her throat just thinking of being trapped down there.

I brought her to the bar and ordered a scotch for me and a martini for her.

"Sit here and wait," I said, turning away before she could ask questions. I wanted a minute to observe her comfort level when she was alone with the threat of men approaching.

There was a man at the end of the bar trying to catch her eye and she ducked her head, letting her hair fall like a curtain to block him from her. The man made a move to approach her and I closed in. She wasn't ready for that yet.

"Hi," I said, sliding into the chair next to her, moving my legs so they blocked her in.

"Hi..." she said uncertainly.

"My name's Chase," I said, extending my hand to her.

Her lips twitched a little as she caught on. "I'm Alexandra Feodorovna," she said, giving me a sweet, innocent smile.

I had to bite the inside of my cheek to keep from laughing, but the smile was beyond my control. "You look damn good for someone who died by firing squad almost a hundred years ago."

"I moisturize," she said, not missing a beat and there was no way to control it, I burst out laughing.

"This isn't going to work if you don't take it seriously," I said as I recovered.

"Sorry. It just... feels weird," she admitted.

"What does? Flirting with me? Baby, I've been *inside* you."

Her mouth fell slightly open. Her pupils dilated. Her thighs pressed together.

"Sorry," I said, not fucking sorry at all. "I didn't mean to get you all hot and bothered."

"I'm not," she said way too quickly for it to be true.

"Really?" I asked, my hand landing high on her thigh. "I could... check that out for you. Just to make sure," I teased, my fingers slipping under the hem of her skirt that had hitched up almost indecently when she sat. If I shifted my fingers the slightest bit, they would make contact with her panties. I would bet everything in my bank account that she was wet for me, right there in the middle of a crowded club. Her body jerked as she felt my finger trace the space where her thighs touched, making her almost fall off the chair. "Okay," I said, pulling my hand away, trying to gain some control. "Sorry." I wasn't sorry at all. "I'll stop." I *needed* to stop.

"I don't want you to stop," she said a little breathlessly.

Fuck me.

God.

She was so fucking sexy and she didn't even know it.

She was going to be the death of me before the night was over.

I leaned closer, letting my mouth get close to her ear. "Believe me babe, I don't want to stop either. I want to drag you out of here, throw you in my car, and watch you ride me until you're screaming my name." She took a shaky breath and pressed her thighs more tightly together. "But I can't do that," I said, letting the words be full of the regret I was feeling. "Tonight you aren't mine to have."

Her eyes flashed and it was gone too soon to see with what, but then she moved away from me so we were no longer touching. "Okay. So what now? You're leaving?"

"No. I'll be here. If you need me, come get me. Or call me. I'll keep an eye on you. If someone is really bothering you..."

"I got it, Chase," she cut me off, her tone a little sharp, leaving me to wonder where I had fucked up again.

"Ava..." I started, my tone soft.

"I said I got it," she said, standing suddenly, grabbing her drink, and moving away from me. She went toward the balcony, looking down into the crowd below. She seemed relatively calm. Meanwhile, I felt like someone had my guts in a vice grip and was twisting them viciously.

It was a sensation that only increased when the man who had been eyeing Ava earlier finally got up the balls to make a move. He was tall and broad with dirty blonde hair. Judging by his suit and the fact that he could afford the VIP lounge, he was well off. Probably secure, confident, experienced.

That was exactly what she needed.

When he led her down to the dance floor, his hand on her hip, I just about lost it.

"Dr. Hudson!" a woman's voice greeted me as I glared at Ava and the guy as they got toward the center of the dance floor.

I tore my eyes away from them and looked over to find Natalie. It was a small fucking world. "Nat," I said, giving her a genuine smile. Shit may have gone south (and in a very nasty way) with us in college, but that was forever ago and we had shared a passionate (albeit tumultuous) relationship for a year. I had just as many fond memories of her as I had bad ones.

She looked good. A little older, a little less plump around the cheekbones, a few creases next to her eyes. Still gorgeous. Tall. Thin. Shapely. Her tits were all but spilling out of her dress which, at twenty-something was flirty, at thirty-something was a little less cute and more like bordering on desperate. Still, it was sexy. *She* was sexy. Time only seemed to make the sexually confident aura she wore around her magnify.

"You look good," she said, looking me up and down. "Time's been kind to you."

"You're as gorgeous as ever, Natalie," I said. It was the simple truth.

"Chasing skirts?" she asked, gesturing to the empty space next to me.

"Working," I said.

"Ah," she said, nodding. "Surrogate thing, right?"

"Yeah."

"Mae really got to you, huh?" she asked, not bothering to sit. She knew it wasn't that kind of run-in.

"It's an important job," I said, shrugging. I wasn't going to betray Mae to Nat. Those two never got along after Nat and I broke up.

"What time will you be done?" she asked, an obvious inflection in her voice.

I could do it.

There would be nothing wrong with it.

I could drop off Ava and call Nat.

I could roll her around the sheets until it took the edge off of my frustration.

I could do it.

But it wasn't right.

It didn't feel right.

"Not tonight, Nat," I said, shaking my head.

Undeterred, she shrugged. "How about I call you and we set something up?"

I glanced over toward the dance floor to see Ava dancing way too close, way too sexually with the lucky asshole who approached her and I felt the vice grip twist again.

"Sure," I said, standing. "Call my office. We'll figure something out."

Then I was gone, tearing down the steps, pushing through the crowd. But I didn't approach. I held myself back, finding some kind of restraint I hadn't been sure I possessed. I leaned against the wall. I watched. I waited. I saw her take more than two drinks. I saw the guy's hands roam over her body. I saw that she didn't flinch away.

Finally, I couldn't fucking take it anymore.

"You're so gorgeous," he told her, rightfully so.

"Thank you," she agreed easily.

"Ava..." I broke in, tone way too stern.

Her entire body stiffened and she untangled herself from her partner.

"She said she ain't with you, bud," the guy broke in. There was steel under his tone that I would have appreciated if she was just another client. He was willing to stand up for her. But she wasn't just any other client.

"She was mistaken. Ava, it's time to go."

Ava stiffened all the more, but refused to turn to look at me. "No. I think I'm good here, Chase. Thanks for your concern. You may leave without me." She sounded like a robot. But her words slurred slightly.

"Ava..."

"I said go, Chase," she snapped.

Really... what choice did I have? I couldn't exactly drag her out of there.

I turned and left.

Not really though.

No fucking way in hell was I just going to leave her alone at a club, drunk, with a guy she didn't know from Adam. I went outside and I waited.

I didn't have to wait long.

It was only a couple of minutes before she burst out of the front doors, moving fast.

"Ava..." I called. Her eyes snapped to mine and they were full of panic. "Hey... babe..." I said, my tone softening automatically. Her eyes stayed on mine for a minute and slowly filled with tears before she turned and started walking in the opposite direction of me. My arm went around her waist before she got two feet away. "It's alright," I murmured, steering her away from the crowd. "Take a breath, Ava," I said as we rounded an abandoned side of the building. She tried, but the air got stuck in her chest. "Hey," I said, pressing her back against the building and cradling her face. "Look at me." Her eyes slid up slowly. "Breathe. You're okay. I'm right here."

The tears brimmed over and slid down her cheeks. She sucked in a breath and leaned against my chest, against her spot, against the safest place in her world. I slid my arms slowly around her.

It wasn't long before she pulled away, wiping her cheeks furiously.

"You alright, baby?"

"Yeah, I... it was too crowded and loud and hot. I couldn't fight it anymore."

"You should have left with me."

Her eyes dropped to my collar. "I was having a good time."

I felt the muscle in my jaw start to tick. "What did you say to your *friend*?"

"I gave him a fake number and I just... ran."

"A fake number, huh?" I asked, smiling. That had a certain someone written all over it. "I'm assuming that was Shay's idea."

"Yeah it's the number of someone she hates."

I felt myself snort as I slipped out of my jacket and placed it around her shoulders. "She's got a good head on her shoulders."

"Yeah. Except she's sleeping with Jake."

There was a bit of bitterness in her voice. "They'll probably be good together," I said, placing a hand on her hip and leading her toward my car.

"They're not together. They're just sleeping together."

"Sure about that?" I asked, smirking. "Those two will be dating in under a week. Mark my words."

"I thought you were a sexologist, not a love expert," she said and I felt my face harden.

"True," I said in a clipped tone as I opened the door for her. That was the damn truth. If I was a love expert, I wouldn't have fucking fallen for a patient. Jesus Christ.

I got behind the wheel and we drove in pained silence until we pulled into the garage where her car was parked. "We have our final session on Monday."

"I know," she said, looking at her hands in her lap.

"Seven."

"As always," she said, getting out of the car.

The door slamming had such a finality to it that I felt it reverberate somewhere deep inside my soul.

After the Session

I went to the group home to counsel the kids.
I helped Eddie skim his walls.
I tried my fucking best to not think about her.
But I thought about her.
A lot.

Tenth Session

Monday came fast. I spent my time wondering what kind of session we would have. I thought about all the ways I could touch her, kiss her, press memories into her skin.

But in the end, I wouldn't be able to do it. To touch her, to kiss her, to be with her. I couldn't do it. Not with knowing that the entire session would feel like goodbye.

I poured myself a drink and sat down in the chair I had for our introductory session, staring unseeingly at the wall for god knew how long.

"Chase..." her voice called softly into the room.

My head turned slowly. "Is it seven already?"

"Yeah," she said, walking toward me. "Are you okay?" she asked, sounding genuinely concerned.

I gave her a humorless smile. "That's my question."

"Well, I'm borrowing it," she said, sitting down across from me.

My hand rubbed across my brow. "You look better."

"Better?" she asked, her brows scrunching together and fuck if I didn't want to kiss her.

"Yeah, I don't know. More like yourself." I sucked in a breath, believing to my core it would be the last chance I would get to say it, "You're beautiful."

Her cheeks went pink and her gaze lowered. "Thank you."

I watched her ducked head. "I figured you wanted a talk therapy session," I said, waving a hand out. Frankly, I didn't know what the hell she wanted. I just knew it was all I could handle.

"Yeah... I... yeah," she stumbled over her words. "How does this go?"

"We can talk about anything you want. How you think therapy went. Any concerns you have for the future..."

"How do you think therapy went?" she asked, wringing her hands.

I sat up slowly, putting my elbows on my knees, making me invade her little space. "Ava, you did so much better than I anticipated."

"Yeah?" she asked, sounding like she needed the validation.

"Yeah baby," I said, then winced at the word. I couldn't call her that anymore. "Yes," I corrected, my tone more firm, professional. "I really wasn't sure we would finish the sessions in the allotted amount of time. You were so withdrawn and timid and then you just... is blossomed too cliché a word?"

"Chase... I can't thank..."

"Don't," I said, the word heavy. "Don't thank me, Ava."

The silence that followed felt weighted. It felt full of things that we needed or wanted to say, but couldn't.

"Ava," I said, before I could think better of it. "Can you come here for a second?" I asked, holding an arm out.

She got up and moved toward my chair then stopped. My hand reached out and pulled her arm toward me. "Closer."

Her eyes rose to mine, a question there. She bit the inside of her cheek before she made the decision and slid onto my lap. I didn't so much as hesitate as I wrapped my arms around her, holding her tightly against my chest. My cheek went down on her hair and I just... held her.

No words were said.

We just did what we were good at- being there for each other.

Her face tilted slightly and she placed a soft kiss against the material of my shirt. I squeezed her tighter as the clock ticked an hour of our lives away, my hand moving up to stroke through her soft hair.

"Chase..." she said quietly.

"Yeah baby?"

She sighed. "You made me so much better."

"No, babe. You made yourself better. I just helped you along."

"Geez, learn to take a compliment, would you?" she asked, trying to lighten the admittedly depressive mood in the room.

I chuckled a little. "You're amazing, Ava. Don't ever let anyone try to convince you otherwise. Promise me that."

"I'll try."

"Not good enough," I said, pressing a kiss to her hair. "Try again."

She snorted, shaking her head at me. "Okay. I'll *really* try."

"You're impossible," I said, a small smile toying with my lips. "In the future when you're with someone and..."

"The moment," she said, cutting me off.

"I'm sorry?"

She tilted her head up to look at me for the first time since she got onto my lap. "Someone once told me to be in the moment," she explained. "I think that was pretty good advice," she said, lying her head back on her spot.

"Okay," I said and the silence fell again.

It wasn't long before we both slowly drifted off to sleep.

Her whole body jolted, jerking me awake. "Hey," I said, my voice sounding rough from sleep. "You alright?"

"Dream," she explained, her head looking toward the clock and then she was pulling out of my arms.

"Where are you going?"

"It's almost one," she said, reaching for her keys and wallet.

"So what?" I asked, sitting forward.

"I just... it's time to go," she said and if I hadn't been so consumed by my own, I might have heard the sadness in her words.

I downed the rest of my scotch to steady my nerves. "I'll walk you to your car."

"No," she said quickly. "No. I'm fine. Stay here. Relax. You look... tired."

I fucking was. Down to my bones.

"Ava..."

"Thank you Chase," she cut me off, moving toward the door quickly and closing it behind her.

I looked at the closed door for a long moment.

So that was it.

She was gone.

Fuck me.

After the Sessions

Twenty Minutes

I got drunk. Too drunk to drive home.

I walked into the bedroom, kicking out of my shoes and moving toward the bed. I fell down into it and climbed under the sheets, rolling onto the side where Ava used to lay.

Which was a mistake.

Because the sheets and pillows smelled like her.

Vanilla.

Sweetness.

Everything I would spend my life missing.

Five Hours

My phone screamed into the silent space, making me spring up in bed and reach for it off the nightstand.

"'Ello?" I said groggily into the receiver.

"Is this Dr. Chase Hudson?" the voice asked and suddenly I was not only sober but more awake than I ever had been before. Because I knew that tone of voice. I knew who used that tone of voice.

"Yes."

"This is St. Mary's hospital," she started and I was already in my shoes and moving through my office.

Fucking fucking fucking Eddie.

"Is he alive?" I barked, not needing the shit they spoon fed all the worried families. I needed the facts. I needed something to either solidify or brush aside the swirling sickness in my stomach.

"Yes, he's alive."

"He overdosed," I guessed as I threw myself into my car.

"I'm afraid so."

"Is he stable?"

"Yes. Unconscious. But yes."

"I'll be there in ten," I said, hanging up the phone.

Alive. Stable.

I walked through the emergency room doors ten minutes later, my feet feeling like cinderblocks were attached to them. Heavy. I fucking felt... heavy.

"Eddie Gregori," I told the nurse at the station.

She glanced down at her paperwork. "Right this way, Dr. Hudson," she said in the somber tone they used for situations like that - when the only fucking person you had in your life OD'd. Again.

People always said loved ones in hospital beds looked small. That had never been true of Eddie. He always seemed to swallow them up. Like they weren't meant for men like him.

He was pale and almost bluish under the lights. But he was still huge. Still healthy looking. Well, that would be true if he didn't have a bunch of tubes sticking out of him. Fluids. A respirator.

"He was brought in an hour ago. The doctor gave him Narcan which he has responded to. He should be back to normal in a bit..." she said, letting her voice sound a little more cheery than was necessary.

"Thanks," I said, moving toward the side of his bed and taking a seat on the stool. I heard her thick soled shoes make their way out of the room and I rested my forearms on Eddie's bed. "You have some timing," I told him, shaking my head.

There was no response. Of course. It wasn't some cheesy movie. It was real life. Loved ones didn't miraculously wake up because you spoke to them. But he *would* wake up. I was going to be there when he did. Then I would be there to guide him back on track. Into rehab. Into outpatient treatment. It didn't matter how many times he dragged me down to the hospital, heart in my throat praying it wasn't the time I would get there and be told he didn't make it. I would be there.

I wondered as I sat at his bedside if it all wasn't just a way for me to try fix the past. I had to save Eddie because I couldn't save my mother. I had to save the kids at the group home because I couldn't save myself. I had to save Ava because I couldn't save Mae.

I hung my head on that heavy thought, listening to the monitor beep out Eddie's heartbeat. It was a hollow kind of comfort. But it was fucking all I had left.

Six Days

I wasn't the kind of man to wallow, to wrap my disappointment and sorrow around myself like a protective barrier. That wasn't me. I knew better. Situations had to be dealt with and then they needed to be moved on from.

So I convinced myself that was what I was doing when I pulled out the number I had written down from my machine at work.

Natalie's number.

Calling her was a way of moving on, of moving past the churning black hole that was taking up residence where my heart used to be.

So I called.

And I set up a date.

Seven Days

I spent the whole next day feeling fucking sick about it. I spent the day feeling like I was betraying Ava.

But I told Mary to let Nat into my office before she left for the night on Monday. I walked her through to the bedroom to pour us drinks, then very pointedly moved her back into my office, closing the bedroom door.

Natalie took in the whole thing with a raised brow, sitting down on the side of my desk and making her skirt hike up on her thigh.

"You've done well for yourself," she said, gesturing around.

"I heard you have as well," I nodded, knowing she had finished school and went back to teach women's studies.

She shrugged away the compliment, sipping her drink. "I was surprised you called," she admitted, watching me.

"Why?"

"Because, Chase, when we were in our twenties, you couldn't keep your hands off of me. Even when we were fighting. It was always an intensely physical relationship. The other night at Chaos... you barely looked me over."

"I noticed you weren't wearing a bra," I countered.

She rolled her eyes, setting her drink on the far end of the desk then cocking one of her legs up on the arm of my chair so her skirt slipped up high. "What color are my panties, Chase?" she asked like a challenge.

And, fuck, she was right.

I didn't even want to look.

"Exactly," she said, putting her leg back down. "So what is going on with you? Because I know I haven't lost it," she said with a confident smirk. "You got yourself a woman?"

I laughed humorlessly, raking a hand through my hair. "No."

"That's not a 'no I don't have a woman', that's a 'a woman has me, but I don't have her'," she told me, a brow raised, daring me to contradict her.

Jesus Christ.

When did I become so easy to read?

"Something like that," I nodded, saluting her with my drink.

"Damn," she said, nodding.

"What?"

"For a shrink, honey, you were always pretty clueless about yourself. You always seemed to think you got out of your shitstorm of a past without scars. Babe, they're all over you. And you have always kept people at arm's length so they couldn't see them."

"Nat..." I said, shaking my head.

"Don't *Nat* me. We dated for a year. We were practically living together for a year. You know how I knew about your mother? Eddie told me when he came over to your place drunk one night while you were at the library. You never once mentioned the fact that you found her body. You never told me that she was bipolar. You never told me that that was why you went into psychology. You never let anyone in on that."

Fuck me.

I let Ava in on that.

Easily.

Like it meant nothing.

I hadn't even thought of hiding it.

"This woman," she pressed, watching me, "does she know about her?"

"Yes."

"So, back to my original statement: *damn*. I never thought I would see the day when you let someone in, Chase. I never thought you would roll up your sleeves and show a woman your damage." She paused, looking at me hard. "What's she like?"

A part of me wanted to tell her, wanted to get it off my fucking chest.

I couldn't.

"She's gone," I said, shrugging. "That's about all there is to know."

Unphased, Natalie rose from my desk. "Want to come to the university next week and be on a panel for my class?" she asked.

"A panel?" I asked, not trusting her tone.

"A panel of men," she clarified with a smirk.

"Will I leave with my balls still attached?" I asked, feeling a smile toying at my lips for the first time in a week.

"I don't know. I have a particularly ruthless class this year. If you give them so much as a hint that you're disagreeing with them, well, no promises," she said, making her way toward the door to the waiting room. I followed her.

"Alright," I said, reaching for the doorknob.

"Thank you so much, *Dr. Hudson,*" she teased in an old, familiar way.

But I wasn't paying attention.

Because the second I opened the door, my eyes found Ava.

She was standing at the reception desk, a big envelope in her hands that she was in the process of putting down.

"Ava?" I asked and even I heard the wonder in my own voice.

Sharp as ever, Natalie didn't miss it either. Her head snapped in Ava's direction and a knowing smirk went to her lips. "I will see you next week," she said, glancing one more time at Ava before she quickly moved to leave.

Ava took the opportunity to drop the envelope and turn to follow the path Natalie had just walked.

"What is this?" I asked and she froze for a second.

She turned slowly, her chin lifted slightly. "*That,*" she said, her tone a little sharp, "is your payment. Which was apparently and, I assume, *mistakenly* canceled."

"You were just going to leave three thousand dollars in cash on the reception desk?"

"You always seem to be... the last one out. I figured you would find it first. But... yeah. So... now you have it," she mumbled, "and I'm... gonna go."

She didn't get a step before I called her. "Ava," I said, and she stilled again. "It wasn't a mistake."

She turned slowly, her face looking guarded. "What?"

"It wasn't a mistake. I am not billing you."

After the night when she called me drunk... yeah the idea of billing her for sessions felt dirty, wrong.

"Why not?"

Christ.

I was going to tell her.

To fucking hell with the consequences.

I ran a hand down my face. "I need a drink," I said, turning back toward my office. I went to the sidebar, mixing drinks, and handed her a martini before I threw back my scotch. "Can you come sit down with me for a minute?" Her eyes went to the couch with what I could only describe as suspicion. I moved over and she chugged her drink before following and sitting down a full cushion away from me. "I'm not billing you."

"You said that. You haven't said why."

"Fuck," I said, rubbing my hand over my brow. How the hell could I even start to explain? I looked back at her, resigned to get it over with when I noticed how red and puffy her eyes looked. "Have you been crying?"

"Chase answer my question," she said, not answering.

"Answer mine," I countered.

She sighed, shaking her head, knowing I wasn't going to back off until she told me. "Not today," she admitted in a small voice.

"Why were you crying at all?" I asked, fighting the urge to reach out and touch her face.

"You already had your question," she said with a slight chin raise.

190

"You're impossible," I said, shaking my head, wanting to smile. "Ava, it would be wrong to bill you for those sessions."

"How would it be wrong? You did what you were supposed to do."

"Yes and no."

"How no?"

"Because I pushed the lines of professionalism." Hell, I fucking plowed over them.

"What because you like... went to my apartment or fed me?"

"Yes, those things but..."

"But what?"

I felt a smile toy with my lips, but shook my head. "Tell me why you were crying first."

Her gaze went to her lap, her hair falling like a curtain to block her from view. "Chase..." she said in a pleading tone.

"Baby, tell me..." I said, my hand landing on her thigh.

She took a slow breath. "Do you remember when I was drunk and you came over and I started blabbering about Dr. Bowler?"

"Something about something being fake. But maybe not. But maybe yes. You were pretty wasted."

She sucked in a breath and looked at my hand as it slid to her knee. "Yeah."

"What was Dr. Bowler right and wrong about?"

"I... went to see her about my sessions with you."

"That was a good idea."

"Yeah, well. I went to see her because I was having some issues..."

"With our sessions?" I asked, feeling like she had stolen my air. She was having issues with me? And I didn't even fucking see it? "Babe... why didn't you tell me?"

"Because I wasn't sure if what I was experiencing was what I thought it was. Dr. Bowler, well, she confirmed it."

"Confirmed what?" I asked, squeezing her knee, feeling my guts twist hard.

"That I had transference."

Jesus Christ.

"Transference," I repeated, my voice an odd croak. "You thought you were having transference?"

"Yeah," she said, swallowing hard. "But, um, it turns out I wasn't."

"Baby, what are you trying to say here?"

"I didn't have transference," she repeated. "I... I was in love with you."

No.

Fucking... no.

That wasn't possible.

Or... was it?

Could it have been mutual?

But one thing struck me...

"Was?" I asked, letting the word hang in the air.

"Am," she corrected and I felt like the swirling black hole just suddenly still in my chest.

She was in love with me.

"You're in love with me?" I asked, needing confirmation.

"Yes."

"*Fuck me,*" I said, closing my eyes tight against the strange current of emotions working their way through my system. "*Fuck me...*"

"Chase..."

My eyes opened slowly to find her perfect face watching me with pure, raw vulnerability. It was something I would never get tired of seeing from her. Because she trusted me with that. She gave me that freely. And I felt so fucking unworthy of it.

"I couldn't bill you, baby, because this wasn't therapy."

"What?" she asked, her brows drawing together.

"I mean... we followed the schedule, but it wasn't therapy."

"What was it then?"

"It was... courting. It was genuine attraction and mutual feelings and..."

"Mutual feelings?" she asked with what sounded like a desperate sort of hope in her voice and I realized I hadn't really *told* her yet.

"Baby... fuck," I said, running my hands down my face. "I knew the second I saw you sitting on my couch that first day that this was different. This wasn't a job. I wanted you. I wanted you more than I have ever wanted anyone. And just how you were. Shy and modest and anxiety ridden. I wanted that girl. And then when you started coming out of your shell around me, letting down your guards, letting me in... I wanted you even more. Every moment with you was like the first time. It was *real,* Ava. It was real for me. It wasn't work."

"Chase... what are..." she started, needing to hear it like I needed to hear it from her.

"I love you, Ava," I said, reaching out to hold her face. "I have never loved anyone. No one. I wasn't even sure I knew what it was until I found you."

Her eyes widened and watered slightly before she whispered, "I love you too, Chase."

My eyes closed as I inhaled. "I never thought I was going to get to hear that. I thought..." I shook my head, not wanting to think about what I had thought anymore. "There was a time when I had hope that you felt the same way."

"When?"

"Anytime I touched you. When you kissed me. When you dressed up for me. When you said my chest was your spot. When you called it the safest place in the world. But I didn't let myself think, or hope, that it was true."

"It was true," she said, giving me a small, sweet smile.

"When did you know?" I asked.

"Around the fourth session. I thought... I thought it was a crush. And then I was sure it was transference. So I spent all my time making sure I understood that you..."

"That I what?"

"Saw me as a patient."

That was the look. The look she gave me anytime I said something that she mistook as professional. *That* was why she looked so pained, yet determined to be cold.

Jesus.

"Never," I said, shaking my head. "Not once. Not for a moment."

Then she was reaching for me, pulling me toward her as her lips sought mine. And we both sank into it, into each other. We kissed with all the frustration, all the misunderstanding, all the time wasted. We kissed hard knowing we had all the time in the world to do so.

My arms went tight around her, lifting her, and bringing her toward the bed. We stood beside it, breaking free just long enough to rip her shirt off of her. Her hands went between us, frantically unbuttoning my shirt and slipping it and my jacket off my shoulders. I sat back, getting free of my belt, pants, and boxer briefs. She got onto the bed, lying against the pillows and my body came down on hers as I tugged her pants and panties down her thighs, legs. Until there was nothing between us anymore.

"I missed you," I said, my words heavy with the truth. "Every day. Every hour. You were all I could think about."

"You too," she admitted.

"So beautiful," I said, leaning down and kissing the space between her breasts before shifting to the side and taking her nipple into my mouth. I sucked the sensitive point and her hips pressed up hard into me. I had to focus to keep myself from burying deep inside her right then and there. I teased her other nipple before moving to kiss a line down her stomach, hungry for a taste of her. But her hands moved out and grabbed my head, pulling me upward. "No?" I asked, brows furrowing.

"No," she said, stroking a hand down my face. "I need you inside me," she said, her legs wrapping around me. "Now."

"Fuck me," I groaned, laying over her, my head pressing down to her forehead as I gained some control.

"Chase... now... please," she begged, sounding just as far gone as I was.

My hips shifted until my cock pressed against her heat. "Fuck... so sweet," I said as she groaned and arched against me. "So wet for me." And, fuck, she was. Dripping.

"Always," she said, her eyes heavy with desire as I started to press inside her.

"God, I like hearing that," I said, leaning down and nipping her lower lip.

Her hands went around me, stroking up my back as I buried deep. "Fuck," I groaned, feeling her tight, wet pussy grab my cock. "You feel so good. But, baby..."

"It's okay," she said softly, her hand moving up to stroke my hair out of my face.

"You're sure?" I asked, praying she was. I wanted nothing between us anymore.

"About ninety-nine percent sure," she said with a small smile. "I want to really *feel you,*" she said, leaning up and kissing my chin.

I felt my eyes close for a second as I rocked my hips into her. "My baby is so fucking perfect," I murmured, my pace slow, gentle.

But not for long. Soon we were both too far gone, too needy to do slow and sweet, and I was slamming into her hard and fast, driving us both toward oblivion.

"Chase..." she gasped as she started to tighten around me.

"Oh... come for me baby," I growled as she pulsated hard around me, taking what was left of my control with her as I slammed hard and buried deep, groaning through my orgasm. "Fuck."

"I love you," she murmured close to my ear as my orgasm slammed through me.

"Fuck... I love you too," I said, riding the last waves.

My weight fell down on her for a second before my strength came back and I rolled us onto our sides, still inside of her.

My hand moved up to stroke her cheek. "I'm done with this," I said, partly to myself.

"With what?"

"This," I said, waving a hand to the room at large. "As of an hour ago. I don't ever want to touch anyone else." And I didn't. It was an easy decision. Nothing had ever felt more right. "I don't think I've ever truly helped anyone until you anyway."

"Chase..."

"I'll keep my practice. But I'm done with surrogacy. It's just you. It's always been you. I just didn't know it until I met you."

She paused a second as the words settled in. "I think you should keep this room, though," she mused, a smile at her lips.

"Oh yeah?" I asked, smiling too. I was thinking the same thing.

"Yeah. We might need somewhere to sneak off to when I take a lunch break."

"That insatiable, huh?" I asked, smiling wider.

"Only for you."

"Come here," I said, rolling onto my back and tapping my chest.

She flew at me and lay on her spot.

The safest place in the world.

The place I always wanted her to be.

Two Weeks

"They're going to think you kidnapped me or something," Ava said, untangling from my arms and moving toward her clothes scattered all over my floor.

"They're too busy with their own thing to even notice you're gone," I said, propping myself up on my arm to watch her ass as she walked away from me.

"For three days?" she countered, looking over her shoulder. Seeing me watching her, she blushed crimson and quickly yanked her panties up her legs.

"I liked the view better without the panties, babe," I said lazily.

"Too bad," she said, an arm crossed over her breasts as she turned toward me to reach for her shirt.

She was getting better about the shyness. Before and directly after sex, I could whip out a camera if I wanted to and she wouldn't even flinch. But it was still new. *We* were new. Her being naked around a man at all was new. She would get there someday. And I wasn't going to push it.

"Shay texted me three times last night," she said, moving back toward the bed and sitting by my feet as she slipped into her shoes.

"We were occupied," I smiled, my mind flashing back to stumbling through the front door, me naked from the waist up because she had been at work with my buttons in the elevator. I took her from behind against the kitchen counter, yanking her

197

pants and panties down to her knees and slamming inside her. Rough. Feral.

"Tell me who your pussy belongs to," I growled into her ear as I yanked her back by her hair.

"You," she said on a moan as my free hand moved down her belly and pressed against her clit. I knew the second I was inside her that it wasn't going to be an all night session. I was too on edge. She was too fucking tight.

"God damn right," I said, thrusting faster as my fingers pressed hard circles around her clit until she came, crying out my name loud enough to wake the neighbors.

Then I yanked her pants and panties up and led her to the bedroom where I stripped her, cleaned her up, then got on my knees and ate her until her legs wobbled so hard that they gave out beneath her.

"Stop looking at me like that," she said, her lips twitching, dragging me out of the memory.

"Like what, babe?" I asked, raising my brows innocently.

"Like you want me again," she said, her gaze dropping away for a second before she looked back at me.

"I do want you again."

"You just had me!" she said, laughing.

And I had. I'd woken up to her kissing my neck and then she rode me slow and soft, making herself come twice.

"I guess it can wait until tonight," I shrugged.

"I'm going *home* tonight," she reminded me unnecessarily.

"Yeah. I was thinking it was about time we broke in that bed too," I nodded and watched her beautiful eyes bug out.

"We can't have *sex,*" she whispered the word like someone might overhear her, "in my bed."

"Why not?"

"Because Shay and Jake share a wall with my room!"

"So?"

198

"So they might hear us!" she said, slapping my leg like I was being unreasonable.

I knifed up toward her, putting my hand over the front of her throat lightly. "Then maybe you'll just have to be a good girl and be very quiet."

Her eyes flashed and she swallowed hard. "I don't know if I can be quiet," she admitted and if the past was anything to go by, she was probably right. But that being said, by the time we got into it, she would forget about sharing a wall with Shay and Jake. Hell, she would forget they fucking existed.

"Sure you can," I said, lying through my teeth.

She exhaled loudly and I knew I had her. "Alright, fine."

Two Weeks & Ten Hours

"I hate you," she said, lowering her eyes at me, her face redder than I had ever seen it as Shay banged her hand on the wall.

"That a girl! You get yours!" she called.

"No you don't," I said, not able to hide my smile as I pulled her toward me. "You love me."

"Not right now I don't," she said, crossing her arms over her chest, trying to hold onto her anger.

"Always," I countered easily.

A knock sounded at the door. "Cover up your naughty bits, I'm coming in," Shay warned and I barely had a chance to flick the sheet over us before the door opened. "You guys might want to, I dunno, put some music on or something," she said, giving me a pointed look that Ava totally missed. "Post-coital pancakes in an hour," she declared, turning and slamming the door and going to 'get hers'.

"Post coital pancakes?" Ava repeated, two small lines between her brows. But then the bed in the other room started slamming on the wall and her mouth fell open. "Oh my god..."

"Music, babe," I laughed and she jumped out of the bed, beautifully naked and not bothering to cover up as she jammed a few buttons on her stereo until it almost, just barely drowned out the racket Shay and Jake were making.

"We're never having sex here again," she grumbled as she climbed back in the bed.

She was wrong about that.

Because after post-coital pancakes, she let me inside her as we spooned. But only because I promised to keep my hand pressed against her mouth the whole time.

<u>Four Months</u>

Ava

"So you're who I have to thank," Eddie said when Chase walked out the door to go grab dinner.

"Thank for what?" I asked, hoisting myself up on Chase's, no... *our*... kitchen counter. The *us* thing had finally stopped feeling odd. But the *our* thing still sent a tiny surge of panic through my system. It wasn't bad per say, just odd. A thrill. Half excitement and half fear. I wondered how long it would take for the fear part to go away. But it had only been two weeks since I officially moved in. I had to give it time.

"For making him happy," Eddie said, moving to stand across from me, making the space feel a little too small and my hand went to my throat where the anxiety felt like it was crushing my windpipe slightly. "He's had a rough life. He deserves a little happiness."

"I agree," I said, thinking how odd it was that the man in front of me and I were the only two people in the world who knew Chase, *really* knew him.

Eddie was a stranger to me still. We had just met fifteen minutes before when Chase brought him in after his stint in rehab. He looked good. I mean... to my untrained eyes. He seemed healthy. Bright-eyed, at ease.

"I know I'm one of the many reasons he's had a rough life..."

"Don't say that..." I started to break in even though I knew it was the truth.

"It's true, honey. We both know it. But, fuck," he said, running a hand through his somewhat shaggy dirty blonde hair. "That night? That night when you left him..." he started and I felt a pain shoot through my chest at the memory. How I felt that night- hopeless, devastated, like I was more screwed up than I had been before. Chase never talked about how he felt that night. He told me that later that night Eddie OD'd and he went to the hospital, but that was it.

"That night..." I prompted, a hand still over my throat, but the pressure was easing slightly.

"Ava, babe..." he said, his eyes holding mine and I saw the grief there. "I'd never seen him like that. He was fucking wrecked."

Wrecked.

I couldn't picture him that way. I didn't *want* to picture him that way.

"I could see it as soon as I opened my eyes. It was like every ounce of happiness was sucked out of him. And trust me, love, he didn't have much in there to begin with. I swore that night that I would never fucking *ever* be a part of making him look like that again."

I felt those words settle deep into my own soul. "Me either," I agreed. "I mean... I, um, I didn't see him like that. But if he felt anything like how I did... I never want to make him feel that way again. I never will."

"I believe you," he said nodding.

The door opened and Chase kicked it closed.

"I believe you too," I whispered so only Eddie could hear.

Chase dumped the bags on the counter, one of his hands automatically going up to where I was holding my throat and pulled it away. "Breathe, baby," he said, kissing my temple as he moved past.

I sucked in a breath.

It was always that easy with him.

Two Years

Ava

"I'm so sorry," I said, hiding my face in my hands to block the tears from view. I shouldn't have been crying. I needed to pull it together. I needed to be strong. For him.

"Baby..." he said, his arm going around my back and crushing me to his chest. His lips kissed the side of my head and he squeezed me tight. "It's okay. You're allowed to cry." He always had to be so nice. So good. So giving. It was all the more reason I needed to pull myself together. "Just stay here with me," he said, taking a deep breath.

I pulled back and looked up at him, handsome as ever in his black suit. Black tie. Black shirt. No buttons. His hands went up and brushed the tears off my cheeks. And I saw it then.

Wrecked.

That was what Eddie had said.

And that was how he looked.

I lifted my chin, feeling my stomach clench painfully at the sight. "I'll be right back," I said, squeezing his hand as I moved up the aisle.

The casket seemed huge. But then again, so was the man inside of it.

He looked silly in a suit.

I had never seen him in a suit before.

It didn't, well, *suit* him.

He should have been buried in jeans and a tee.

I lowered myself onto the bench beside the casket, laying my hands on the side.

"*I believed you,*" I hissed, surprised to feel the anger well up strong and unstoppable. "We stood in that kitchen and we made promises. And I *believed* you," I said, the tears flowing freely. "And now he has that look, Eddie. He has that look he had that night that you said you would never put on his face again."

It felt wrong to be angry at a dead person.

But then again, it felt wrong for Eddie to *be* a dead person.

When we had walked up to find a bunch of Eddie's work buddies laughing and joking and Chase had felt me tense, he ran a hand up my back and murmured in my ear, "There's no wrong way to grieve, baby."

So I was allowed to be angry.

Even at a dead person.

As soon as I acknowledged that right, though, the anger drained away... leaving only the sadness. Sadness because he was a good man. He had been a good brother to Chase, a good friend to me. He had made me laugh over dinner hard enough for wine to come out of my nose. And he hadn't teased me about it. At Christmas when we were all decorating a tree, he had knelt down in front of me and told me to climb on. Then he hoisted me up like a kid so I could put the star on the top.

Sadness because he was such a good man, but so full of demons that the only way he could deal with them was to drown them at the bottom of bottles or in pills or powder or whatever else he got himself into.

"I'm really going to miss you," I said, standing up, wiping my eyes, and making my way back to my man with tears still clinging to my lashes.

I found him standing toward the back of the room, his hand on a redhead's arm, giving her a small smile. The redhead was tense, her gaze on Chase's hand on her arm. And I recognized that look. Panic. Fear. Chase noticed too, squeezing her forearm slightly before letting his hand drop. "Ava," he breathed when he saw me, his arm sliding across my hips. He leaned down and kissed my nose before turning back to the woman. "Ava, this is Mae."

<u>Three Years</u>

Chase

At first, it was wrong to ask her. Because she was still struggling to settle in, still jumpy. Still worried like she was constantly waiting for the other shoe to drop.

When that finally went away, well, Eddie died.

And we both needed to grieve.

But it was time.

Three years.

Three years I spent every night with her resting on my chest. And I wanted to make damn sure she knew that that was where she belonged. Forever.

My hand went into my pocket, worrying the small blue case as I waited.

She was late.

205

I still smiled every fucking time she was.

Because it was a reminder of how far she had come, how comfortable she had gotten with me.

"Why would you have me come all the way to your office when we could just meet at Jake and Shay's?" she asked from the doorway, making me jump almost guiltily.

"Come over here, baby," I said, holding out an arm.

"We're going to be late."

"Don't worry about it. They'll understand," I said, pulling her toward the seating alcove and pressing her into the couch as I took the chair across from her.

A smile toyed at her lips. "Am I suddenly in need of some therapy?" she asked playfully.

"It all started here," I said, ignoring her comment.

"What?" she asked, her head tilting.

"Us," I clarified. "It all started right here."

"Oh my god," she said, realization crossing her face, making her pale slightly.

"Jake and Shay will be okay with us being late," I repeated, reaching into my pocket. "Because I need to ask you something," I said, sliding down by her feet.

"Oh my god," she said again, her hand closing over her throat.

I pushed open the box, taking out the platinum band with a princess cut diamond. "Breathe, baby," I said as I took her hand from her throat and slowly slid my ring on her finger. She sucked in a shaky breath. "Will you marry me?" I asked simply, having spent the last month trying to think of what to say when I asked her. But in the end, she didn't want flowery words and I just needed an answer.

But she didn't say yes.

No.

She flung herself at me, sending us both falling backward as I wrapped my arms around her and her head rested on my chest. "It's mine," she declared.

"What is?" I asked, squeezing her.

"My safest place in the world," she said, lifting her head from it. "It's mine forever."

My hand went to the side of her face. "It always has been," I told her.

"I love you, Chase."

"I love you too, baby," I said, wrapping her tight as I knifed up and walked her toward the bedroom.

We were late at Shay and Jake's.

Very late.

"Let's see it!" Shay shouted across the crowded apartment where Ava used to live.

A shy smile spread over Ava's face as she held out her hand.

"Damnnnn girl," Shay said, nodding at her. "About time, Dr. Sex," she said, turning to look at me. "Now if *someone*," she declared loudly so everyone in the room could hear, "would take a damn hint and slip one of those on *my* finger, all would be right in this world."

"Woman," Jake said, making his way toward us, "you turned me down," he reminded her, rolling his eyes at us.

"I was fat!" she said, eyes wide like he had completely lost his mind.

"You were pregnant," he corrected, putting an arm around her waist, the arm that wasn't holding their eight month old son.

"Yeah. And my stomach looked like I swallowed a god damn basketball. I wasn't getting married like that. I want to be able to see my feet in their kickass heels when I am walking down the aisle."

Ava laughed, shaking her head at them like she always did as she reached to pull the baby out of Jake's arm.

"Hey buddy," she said, jiggling him against her hip.

I felt my eyes looking at her hard, liking what I saw way too much.

"You'll make a cute one," Shay said as if sensing where my mind was heading. "Not as cute as Ranger. Everyone knows mixed babies are the cutest. But cute," she winked and led Jake away.

"What?" Ava said, noticing me watching her.

Oh yeah. I was going to marry her.

Then I was going to get my baby inside her.

"I love you, baby," I said instead, snaking my arm around her.

She looked up at me for a long minute then burst out laughing.

I smiled, touching her cheek. "What?" I asked when she got a hold of herself.

She shook her head at herself.

"Thank god I was such a mess, huh?" she asked.

I snorted, nodding. "Yeah, baby. Thank god you were such a mess."

"And thank god you didn't end up having moobs or meat hands."

I laughed, my brows drawing together. "Was that a possibility?"

"Well it seemed a lot more likely than a cover model walking into that office."

"A cover model?" I smirked, my brow raising.

"Oh, shut up and learn to take the compliment, would you?" she said, leaning into me.

"Okay, baby."

She paused, turning her head to kiss my chest.

"I love you too, Chase."

Fuck me.

xx

208

BONUS: The Wedding

- Ava -

"I'm not going to freak out. I. Am. Not. Going. To. Freak. Out."

Okay. I was freaking out. As in, my stomach had wedged itself somehow into my esophagus and I felt perpetually sweaty and cold at the same time. Oh, and that stomach in the throat thing? Yeah, well, it was making it really hard to breathe. Meaning... I couldn't. It wasn't that I didn't want it. Oh, my god, how I wanted it. I wanted it more than anything else in the world. To be married to Dr. Chase Hudson? Hell freaking yes. You'd have to be, well, a lesbian or asexual or something to not want that. I wasn't a lesbian. And I wasn't asexual. So, yeah, I wanted to marry him. In fact, it had been the only thing on my mind since he had asked me eight months before. Eight months of thinking about him watching me walk down an aisle, of him lifting my veil, of him slipping his ring on my finger while making me promises I knew he would keep, of him pulling me up against his chest, my safest place in the world, and kissing me to seal the deal.

But, well, somehow I had managed to not think about the fact that it wouldn't just be him watching me walk down the aisle.

No.

There was going to be an entire room full of people who would watch me walk down the aisle.

And, knowing me, I would probably trip and make an idiot of myself. I would likely stutter and stammer my way through my vows. Or, oh god, go mute. Jesus. That could totally happen. Granted, it hadn't happened in almost two years. But still, it was a possibility.

"Shit. Oh, shit shit shit," I groaned, pacing the floor in Shay and Jake's apartment, careful not to step on any of the eleven-million toys that belonged to a very recently mobile sixteen-month-old Ranger.

"Girl, you need a drink," Shay said, watching me as she leaned against my old bedroom door that now belonged to Ranger, her arms crossed over her chest. "It's ten o'clock in the morning," I protested, stepping on a stuffed dinosaur that let out a high-pitched squeal. I winced, turning back to Shay. "Sorry," I said, knowing it just took her twenty minutes, three bedtime stories, and two songs to get Ranger to finally settle down.

Shay waved a hand. "He starts crying, he's his father's problem," she said, moving across the living room to the locked liquor cabinet. "And, sure, it's ten in the morning. But it is ten in the morning on your wedding day. You're allowed to have a shot of tequila to calm your nerves."

"I think I need an elephant tranquilizer to calm my nerves," I said, but accepted the shot and threw it back, letting it burn its way down and settle with a warm feeling in my stomach.

"You love Dr. Sex," Shay said.

"Yes." "He loves you."

"Yes." He did. Oh, god he did. It still felt wondrous to realize that, to know that the sweetest, sexiest, and well... yummiest man I had ever met actually loved shy, stumbling, bumbling me.

"He wants you to put on a white dress, walk down an aisle, and promise to be his forever."

"Yes." Damn her and her rationality.

"He wants to put another ring on your finger and he wants to give you his last name."

Ava Hudson.

Mrs. Hudson.

Okay. I felt like a middle schooler scribbling her name and her crush's name on her notebook. But, damn, Ava Hudson did sound good.

"Yes."

"Then he wants to lay a big wet one on you- staking his claim in front of everyone you know."

Everyone you know. Oh, god. I made a weird croaking sound, sitting down on the couch and cradling my head in my hands.

"Jesus, Shay, what the fuck did you do?" Jake asked, coming out from the shower with a towel slung low on his hips.

It had been so long since I lived with him. I forgot how comfortable he was with his own near (or full) nudity. Not that he didn't have the body for it, he totally did. But still. It was weird. For three years, the only man I had seen nearly (and fully) naked was Chase. I felt a blush creep up on my cheeks as I glanced away from him.

"What are you talking about? I didn't do anything," Shay objected, raising a brow.

"She's more freaked out than she was when I went into the shower," Jake pressed, moving over and sitting down next to me (I repeat... sitting down on the couch next to me. In a towel. Still glistening from the shower).

"That isn't my fault. People gettin' married get jitters. Ava, being Ava, gets full on fucking end of the world panic attacks."

"Fuck, Shay, she's sitting right here," Jake said, big-eyeing her to try to get his point across.

"What? She knows she's a mess. Right?" she asked, addressing me.

"Right," I agreed because, well, I was a mess.

"Should we call Chase?" Jake asked.

"What? No!" I screeched, my voice reaching hysterical proportions. They couldn't call Chase. They couldn't tell him that I was freaking out about marrying him. I didn't want him getting the wrong idea. I totally, absolutely wanted to marry him. Just... you know... in private. With like just the two of us. And a preacher. Hell, the preacher was even negotiable. Why couldn't people just marry themselves?

"Ava," Jake said, snapping me out of my own little internal freak out.

"Yeah?" I asked, deep breathing. "Let me call Chase. He can talk you down."

So Jake had a bit of a man-crush on Chase. Most days, I found it kind of endearing. Jake had this whole looking up to Chase like a big brother thing going on and it was sweet. But Jake also sort of believed that Chase could fix everything. That, apparently, included his anxiety-ridden fiancée on their wedding day. But this was one thing I couldn't let Chase fix. I needed to get myself together.

"No," I said, making my voice even. "No. I've got this. I'll be fine."

"See? She says she's fine. Now go get your suit on and get over there and take care of the groom. I got the bride," Shay said, nodding for emphasis.

Jake stood, shrugging. "I'll bring Ranger so you two hens can cluck and talk about wedding night lingerie, or blow job tips, or whatever the fuck chicks talk about."

212

"His suit is hanging on the back of the door," Shay said, completely breezing past the lingerie and blow job comment, as was her nature.

"You know, I think now that he's walking, he can totally be the ring bearer." "He'd swallow or drop the rings," Shay said, rolling her eyes.

"So we put them on a chain around his neck or something."

"Like those freaks do when they have their dogs be the ring bearers?" Shay asked, eyes bugging and I could feel an argument brewing. "Our son is not a fucking dog."

"Oh for fuck's sake, woman. It was just an idea. There's already no flower girl. I thought..." I blocked out the rest of the good-natured bickering because, well, the blood was rushing through my ears. But I did notice Jake smiling behind Shay's back as she flung her hands out, pacing around the kitchen, getting herself nice and worked up. He liked her worked up because the make-up sex was off the charts. I knew that because Shay told me. It was the reason she didn't mind all the arguing either.

When she told me, I half wanted to pick a fight with Chase just to see if it worked for us too, but I never got up the courage. I walked through my old apartment, familiar but somehow not as well, making my way to the bathroom and taking a long, scalding hot shower which in no way lessened my nerves.

But I was hellbent on going through the motions as if I wasn't inwardly wondering how pissed Chase would be if he got a call from me from, say, Bora Bora, lounging on the beach and drinking myself silly on whatever local drink the Bora Borians (was that what they were called?) drank. I figured he wouldn't be pissed at all, just worried. That only made me feel guilty for even thinking it as I carefully blew my hair straight and slipped into the gaudy hot pink tracksuit that Shay got specially made with "Property of Chase" written across the ass. I had every plan of tying the zip-up shirt across the hips.

Granted, it had the same phrase across the boobs of the t-shirt I had to wear underneath, but I figured that was slightly less embarrassing than having it on my butt.

"Girl, let me in," Shay said, knocking on the door. I opened it to find her holding out a drink to me, already sipping from her own. "More jitter juice," she said, not looking away until I took a long swig. When Shay said 'juice,' she meant a splash of cranberry and about a cup and a half of vodka. It burned in all the wrong ways, but after a few minutes, I felt myself calming marginally.

"We doing your makeup here or at the hall?"

"Hall," I decided, thinking it would probably be a good idea to get my ass there before I started taking the Bora Bora idea seriously. Once I got to the hall, there was no way I could sneak out without creating a huge scene which was almost (but not quite) as terrifying as the idea of the ceremony.

"Aight," Shay said, finishing her drink and grabbing her makeup bag (and by 'bag' I meant 'suitcase') off the counter. "Let's get a move on. Our dresses should be there. Let's go get you married to Dr. Sex already."

- Chase -

"She's freaking out, isn't she?" I asked as Jake made a grab for Ranger who thought my record collection looked like Frisbees.

"Ah," Jake said, looking torn.

"She's freaking out," I concluded, knowing he didn't want to break Ava's trust (or get on Shay's shit list).

I wasn't surprised. If anything, I was surprised it took her so long to start spiraling. All night last night she had been calm as a cucumber, prattling on about scuba diving and wind surfing. I had no fucking plans on scuba diving or wind surfing, planning instead on spending every waking moment buried deep inside her- on the beach, in the pool, in the hot tub, on the pier, so I kept my mouth shut and let her talk.

She woke up early, gave me a pre- tooth brushing close-mouthed kiss, and told me she had to get to Shay's. Not a hint of anxiety.

I should have known. But even if I had, there's no way she would have talked to me about it. She would think that I would think that she didn't want to marry me. Which was ridiculous. She did. I knew she did. She would just prefer if we could do it at the Justice of the Peace. I could have given that to her. It would have been the kinder, more understanding thing to do.

But the fact of the matter was, I didn't want small and private. I wanted the whole fucking world to know that I was marrying her. I wanted everyone I knew and cared about to see her in a white dress, giving herself to me. It was selfish, but it was something I wasn't willing to give in on. Not that Ava would have fought me on it.

"Is is bad?" I asked.

"Depends on your definition of bad," Jake said, shrugging.

He was one of the few people who understood her scale of panic as well as I did, having lived with her for so long himself. While I had written him off at first as a clueless roommate, he had actually paid a fair amount of attention to her. "Is it as bad as that first night you two slept together or how bad she was when your sessions were over? No. She's somewhere around when she first figured out she had feelings for you. I dunno... a six or seven."

Six or seven wasn't bad. It wasn't good, but at least she wasn't a flight risk.

"Alright," I said, checking my pocket for the rings for the fifth time. "Shay texted that they were on their way to the hall like fifteen minutes ago. Figure that's a step in the right direction." He hefted Ranger up onto one of his shoulders, a hand at his belly and a hand at his back.

"Think she's gonna walk into the room, see all those people, and dart?"

Leave it to Jake to be blunt.

"Well," I said, grabbing my keys, "only one way to find out."

- Ava -

Okay. It was okay. I sat down at the vanity as Shay flounced (yes, flounced) around me, mascara wand at the ready.

"I really think we should revisit the fake eyelash idea. Just a couple individuals even."

"Chase doesn't like fake eyelashes," I said, thinking of the time he took me to a club while we were still doctor/patient and I had worn them. He had accused me of not looking like me. As much as I maybe didn't want to be me right then and there, getting ready for my ceremony, I certainly wanted to look like me. For Chase.

"Men don't notice shit like fake eyelashes," Shay insisted, tucking the mascara away and reaching for something that was apparently going to give me a 'dewy' look.

"Chase does." Chase noticed everything.

One morning, two months into dating, I had gotten my period, but hadn't said anything because, well, ick, but I had pressed my hand to my crampy belly as I sipped my much-needed coffee. He noticed. He noticed and then he came home with a selection of chocolate bars and a huge greasy delicious pizza. Then, later that night, he had snuggled me as I curled up with my heating pad.

God, but I did want to marry him.

The door swung open and my eyes landed on Jake who was shaking his head.

"Your mother is here," he said in the tone he reserved for situations he was trying to ease me into. "She wants to come in and see the bride. Her words, not mine," he said, shaking his head at me.

"Oh god," I groaned.

Okay.

I loved my mom.

I did.

That being said, my mother was a bit, well, much. As in, I needed to move two states away from her to keep her from dropping in every other day and lecturing me about needing to shake off the anxiety, find myself a man, and settle down. It went without saying that she was beyond happy that I had landed myself a guy ('a doctor, no less!') and might give her some much hinted at (read: badgered me about) grand babies.

I looked up to Shay with my big eyes and she gave me a shrug.

"She's your mom. It's your wedding day. You have to let her in."

Damn it. She was right.

"Am I done?" I asked, gesturing toward my face. Shay stepped back, head tilted to the side, giving me a serious inspection.

"Yeah, you're done."

I attempted a deep breath, but it got caught a bit on the end. "Alright. Send her in," I said, nodding at Jake as Shay followed him to the door.

Ready or not.

"I never thought I'd see the day when little Anxious Ava walked down an aisle!" my mom said, bursting in, arms spread, smile huge. Yeah, um, definitely not ready. The stomach in the throat thing came back, stronger, feeling like it was completely cutting off my airway.

My hand moved up to my throat as my mother rushed toward me, kissing my cheeks, and pulling an ottoman over to sit on in front of me. She was talking, but I wasn't listening over the whooshing sound in my ears and the suddenly quite alarming slamming of my pulse in my throat, temples, and wrists. Bora Bora. I needed to freaking get to Bora Bora. Right that minute.

- Chase -

Mae walked up to me, a huge smile on her face.

"You look nice," she said, reaching out and squeezing my arm. It was the closest to a hug she would ever get. I learned, after Ava kept pressing the issue, to stop trying to convince Mae that she should give dating a try. If she said she was content, fulfilled, happy, then who was I to say otherwise?

"Thanks for coming Mae," I said, giving her a small smile.

"Of course. I would never miss this. I love Ava. And I love you two together. You're good for each other." Yeah we were. "I'm sorry Eddie isn't around to see this," she said, making me visibly start.

It wasn't that he hadn't been on my mind on and off all day, he had, but hearing someone else call it, it made the dull ache suddenly sharpen.

"He would have been so proud to stand up with you."

He would have, but there were simply some things that could never be.

"I have someone standing up with me," I said, nodding over her shoulder at Jake who was making a beeline toward me, a slight tightness around his eyes that didn't belong there. I'd made the decision to have Jake be my best man for several reasons: One, because while I was close with a few of my other foster brothers, no one came close to how tight I was with Eddie. Two, Jake was Ava's friend. As such, we spent a lot of time together, getting to know one another, sharing a part of our lives. Three, well, I figured Ava would be less spooked to walk up to me if I didn't have a virtual stranger standing with me.

"What's up, Jake?" I asked as he rounded on Mae, giving her a small smile.

"Just figured I'd let you know that Ava's mom has her cornered in her dressing room. She's, ah, not exactly happy about it." More like she was on the verge of bolting.

"Jake, can you show Mae to her seat?" I asked, watching as he nodded, gave her one of his old playboy smiles, and offered her his arm. I felt myself straighten as I watched Mae do the same. She didn't do physical contact with men. She hardly allowed my hand on her arm. She almost never reached out to touch me. That wasn't her. She simply didn't do that. And she had known me since she was eighteen.

But then the strangest thing happened, after only the briefest of hesitations, Mae wrapped her hand around Jake's arm and let him lead her away. I paused to watch for a minute before shaking it off to be thought about at another time as I made my way toward Ava's dressing room.

I liked Ava's mom. She was sweet and welcoming and always had Ava's best interest at heart.

That being said, she was very in-your-face and emphatic, always making Ava tuck herself back inside her shell like a little girl. Knowing that Ava was already struggling, having her mom cornering her and saying god-knew what, well that was simply a recipe for disaster... and me standing alone at the altar. I knocked softly but went in without waiting for a response.

"Oh, Chase!" her mother said, hopping up off her ottoman and walking toward me, all smiles.

"Hey, Cathy," I said, letting her rub her cheek against mine.

"Mind if I have a minute with Ava?"

"Isn't it bad luck?" she asked, lowering her eyes at me.

"Not if she's not in her dress," I said, leading her none-too-subtly toward the door.

"Oh, alright," she said as I stood in the doorway.

"Have Jake lead you to your seat," I suggested.

"Oh, that boy," she said with a motherly smile before touching my cheek and moving away.

I closed the door, twisting the lock, before turning back to look at Ava.

Her hand was at her throat, fingers digging into the delicate flesh. My ring was on that hand, the diamond flashing brilliantly. I moved over toward her, taking up the ottoman her mother had vacated.

"Ava, baby," I said, reaching for her hand and pulling it away from her throat, seeing the little crescent-shaped indentations in her skin. "Breathe, okay?"

Her brown eyes found my face, but they were wide and panicked. "I want to marry you!" she said, almost hysterically.

"I know you do, sweetheart," I said, squeezing her hand.

"But I really, really want to be in Bora Bora right now."

I felt my brows draw together as I fought the twitching of my lips. "Bora Bora?"

"With a lot of alcohol," she clarified, sucking in a shallow breath.

I let the smile spread on my face as I reached my free hand out to stroke her cheek. "Tomorrow at this time, baby, we will be on a beach and you can have all the alcohol you want."

"That doesn't help me in this moment, though, does it?" she asked, rolling her eyes at me.

I chuckled, shaking my head.

"Alright, enough of that," I said, reached out for her and hauling her toward me until her knees landed on either side of my hips.

"Chase, what are you..." she started to object when there was a loud banging on the door.

"Not now," I growled, feeling Ava squirm around on top of me, trying to move away, a blush creeping up on her cheeks.

"Chase?" Shay's voice called, sounding a mix of surprised and amused.

"Give us half an hour, Shay," I called back. A half an hour was not nearly enough time for what I had planned, but it was going to have to do.

"You need to be at the altar in twenty. I need to get her dressed in fifteen."

"Fine. Fifteen," I said through gritted teeth. I could hear Shay laugh.

"That's one way to calm her down," she said and I heard her retreat.

"Calm me down?" Ava asked, brows drawing together.

"Mmhmm," I murmured, reaching out to stroke her hair off her neck and letting my lips land there.

"Oh," she murmured, already sounding breathless.

"Yeah," I said, smiling against her neck, "oh."

- Ava -

His hands moved to my hips, pressing them down to his lap so I could feel his cock straining against his slacks. My hips moved of their own volition, rubbing against his hardness. It didn't take much. With Chase, it was always easy. All he had to do was chuckle, look at me with those soft eyes, call me pet names, breathe... exist. I was always ready for him.

There were times, quiet moments here and there, when I still marveled at how far I had come, how different I was. Not fixed. There were more miracles in mental illness. But I was better. I was calmer, more confident. I didn't just suffer through physical contact, I reveled in it. I couldn't get enough.

Chase gave that to me. I took it. Happily. Frequently. And, apparently, that also meant in my dressing room in my wedding hall on my wedding day. In fact, twenty minutes before I was meant to walk down an aisle.

Old Anxious Ava wouldn't have been able to even think that thought, let alone let her head fall back on a sigh as Chase's tongue slid down the side of her neck.

New, improved, though not perfect Ava? Yeah, she was loving it.

"You wet for me, baby?" he asked, tilting his head to look up at me.

"Always," I said honestly, my hand running over the scruff on his cheek, the scruff I had expressly asked him not to shave for the ceremony. I gave him no fake eyelashes Ava- his Ava. He gave me no shave for three days Chase – my Chase.

"Thank Christ," he said, pushing me up until I stood.

His hands wasted no time, going to the waistband of my pants and pulling them and my panties down. "I have fifteen minutes to make you come hard enough to forget that anything in this world exists besides me and my cock."

Well then.

Okay.

His hand grabbed my knee, pulled it up on the ottoman, cocked to the side, and used his other hand to grab my ass and pull me forward toward him. Toward his mouth. His tongue slipped up my cleft, finding my clit quickly and working over it in small circular swipes until my thighs started shaking so hard that I had to put my hands down on his shoulders and press to hold up my own weight.

His hand moved up between us and slipped inside, curling, stroking over my G-spot with practiced perfection.

"Oh my god," I groaned, my fingers digging into his shoulders. Close. I was so close. "No!" I shrieked when he pulled away, a devilish smile playing at his lips as he suddenly knifed up, grabbed me, and pushed me down onto the ottoman.

My forearms hit it as I let out a quiet 'humph' at the impact.

Chase's hands sank into my hipbones hollows, using them to drag my ass upward toward him. I was released, heard a zip, felt a rush of wetness pool between my legs in anticipation.

"Touch yourself for me, baby," he commanded and my hand moved between my thighs without hesitation. He made a growling sound and I knew he was watching me work my clit like he had just done with his tongue. "Good girl," he said, the palm of his hand kneading my ass for a moment as he watched.

"Better hold on, baby," he warned and my hands moved out to grab the edge of the ottoman. Chase could (and did) give it to me a lot of ways. We made love. We teased. We had kinky, inventive sex. But when Chase wanted to fuck, he meant hard. When he told me to hold on, he meant I would be off the ottoman and on the floor if I didn't. So I held the hell on. "Give it to me, Ava," he said and I could feel as he shifted his cock toward me. I arched my ass up to him like he wanted and his cock slid up my cleft to my clit, pressing hard, before moving down to the entrance, pausing, then slamming inside to the hilt. Nothing, nothing in the world would ever feel as good as he felt inside me.

"Fucking perfect," he growled, his hand snaking up my back to slip into my hair, twisting close to the root and pulling. It didn't even occur to me to tell him not to ruin my hair for the wedding pictures. All I could think was *harder*. Then, as if reading my thoughts, he pulled harder. His cock slammed into me over and over, hitting deep, arching up, giving me that delicious pinch that drove me closer and closer to the edge.

"That's it," he said, his voice gravely, "come for me."

I bit into my lip, trying to keep myself from screaming out his name (I will add that I failed miserably at this) as my orgasm ripped violently through my system, a fast, deep pulsating sensation that felt never ending.

Chase thrust through until my body felt languid, spent.

The hand not in my hair clamped down on my shoulder, pulling me backward as he slammed forward, buried deep, and growled out my name.

"Fuck baby," he said a moment later, moving away from me and I fell full-body onto the ottoman.

I heard a zip and the sound of water running before he came back to me, rolled me unto my back, and cleaned me up.

He moved away again and I finally had the presence of mind to yank up my panties and pants before he came back to sit next to my body, looking down at me.

"Next time I'm inside you," he said, his eyes going soft and I felt my heart skip, "you're going to be my wife." His hand moved to my cheek, stroking across it lovingly. "So I am going to send Shay in here to get you in your dress and you are going to walk down the aisle to me, looking at me how you're looking at me right now..."

"How am I looking at you?" I asked, not able to help myself. His lips turned up slightly as his thumb stroked over my lips.

"Like I'm the only fucking man in the world."

My heart swelled in my chest as my hand wrapped itself around his wrist, squeezing.

"You look at me like I'm the only woman in the world," I said, because it was true.

"Baby, you are," he said simply, moving to stand up. "I'll see you in fifteen minutes, yeah?"

I titled my head to watch him stand in the doorway and, just like that, the anxiety slipped away.

"Yeah," I agreed on a meaningful whisper.

"Fuck me," he said, giving me a lip twitch and then he was gone. I barely got two minutes before the door flew open and Shay slammed it shut, locking it, while somehow simultaneously whipping her shirt off. She was halfway out of her pants as she grabbed her bridesmaid dress (black, tight, tasteful with a hint of slut. Shay had picked it, obviously).

"Thank god he can give it to you fast because now we have to fix whatever damage he did to your makeup and," she said, snapping the strap into place on her shoulder as she finally looked down at me, "your hair," she said, with a head shake and a knowing smile. "Guess you ain't done with all that sex therapy," she mused, laughing.

I looked up at the ceiling, my hand going to my heart that felt a little too big for my chest, and I smiled. Huge.

- Chase -

Ava had planned things perfectly.

Well, perhaps it was more accurate to say that Shay did, seeing as those two worked out the arrangements together and when Shay was involved, 'together' usually meant that Ava sat somewhere nearby, shell shocked by the aggressive certainty Shay approached everything in life. Whoever did it, it was perfect, simple, elegant.

The formal white material draped chairs had been removed and replaced with rustic wooden ones. The ones lining the aisle had simple white bows attached to the side with a few white flowers sticking out. The alter was draped with white curtains tied with the same bows and flowers as the chairs. Nothing crazy. Nothing overstated. But beautiful.

Shay may have planned it, but it had Ava written all over it.

Jake walked up behind me, clamping a reassuring hand on my shoulder for a moment as the music slowly started to play and Shay appeared in the doorway.

Ava insisted on not having a typical wedding party. She wanted Shay, I wanted Jake, so that was all we had.

Shay looked gorgeous as always, her black dress hugging her in all the right places and it was obvious she had been the one to pick it out. She kept her makeup simple and held simply three of the flowers that matched all the others in the room, tied with a white bow. She winked at me as she got close, gave Jake a rare soft look, and moved to her position across from me, half turned to watch the aisle.

I turned as well as the music changed. It wasn't *The Wedding March* like Shay had tried to insist because Ava had surprisingly (and quite stubbornly) stood her ground about it.

It was a classical version of the song that had played when I first made love to her. When I found that out, I had spent the entire fucking night showing her how much I appreciated her remembering things like that. I didn't know how most grooms felt waiting for their fiancées to step into that doorway, but I knew how I felt.

I felt an overwhelming sense of comfort.

I felt my heart pick up its pace, but in excitement, not anxiety.

Everything felt so fucking right.

Then a visibly shaking Ava stepped into the doorway, hands clenched so tight around her flowers that her skin had went white.

All I could think was: perfect. She was fucking perfect.

Her gown was simple, as I would have expected. It had small straps and a low but tame cut over the bust, tight, then flaring out in some kind of whispy material that seemed to float around her as she took her first two tentative steps into the room.

Her eyes were on me, wide, panicked, but she was moving.

She was halfway down the aisle when I lost her eyes. Her gaze moved from me to Shay, then Jake, then away toward the crowd. And she froze. As in *froze*. She stopped dead in the center of the aisle, looking around, her breath catching and she made no effort to try to suck in any air.

Fuck.

I knew I was supposed to stand there, wait for her to come to me. That was how it worked. But I also knew that there was no way in fucking hell I could watch her struggling and do nothing.

I didn't even register the odd looks from our audience as I moved off the altar and made my way up the aisle toward her.

Her eyes were glued to her mother who was giving her huge, disbelieving eyes.

"Baby," I said, my hand moving to the side of her neck and her gaze snapped to mine at the contact. "Breathe," I reminded her.

Her hands fell to her sides as she flung herself at my chest, her face resting against her safest place in the world as my arms went around her and squeezed her tight.

"I'm so so so so sorry," she murmured against my suit, her voice shaky.

"For what?" I asked, my hands moving up and down her spine. "You're here, marrying me."

"You're not supposed to have to come and pull me down the aisle," she said, quietly enough for only me to hear.

Around us, the music paused then started again and I knew that was Shay's doing. She was giving us our moment without things getting too awkward.

"I'm not dragging you down the aisle," I murmured against the side of her hair.

"I am hugging my beautiful fiancée before I slip my ring on her finger."

Her arms squeezed me tighter as she finally took a deep breath.

I waited for her to take another before I loosened my hold enough to be able to look down at her.

"You gonna come and marry me?" I asked, giving her a small smile.

Her cheeks went a little pink as she gave me a shy, slightly wobbly smile.

"I love you," she said simply, but the words were heavy. They always were when she said them.

"I love you too, baby," I said and my words were heavy too, like they always were. Her arms fell from around me and I let mine fall as well, clasping her hand and leading her the last few feet to the altar.

She offered the minister a tight smile before her eyes fell on me and never looked away, like I was the only man in the world, because to her, I was. And now I always would be.

- Ava -

"You may now kiss the bride."

A slow, devilish smile spread across Chase's face and I knew I was in for it: a big, wet, whopper of a kiss, right in front of everyone the two of us knew. And, strangely, with the weight of his band on my finger, I couldn't care less about our audience.

He reached for me slowly, one of his hands snaking across my hips, the other moving to grab the side of my neck. As soon as he had a hold, he hauled me against his body, my hands slamming into his shoulders as he held me plastered to him, looking down at me with soft eyes a moment before they heated and he crushed his lips down to mine.

It was a kiss that seared, that made me forget where I ended and he started, that made time stand still, that made me forget anything else existed in the entire universe. It was a kiss that made me his, forever, and made him mine, forever.

He led me back down the aisle, people cheering and clapping and wishing us well. I heard none of it. I had eyes and ears and body only for Chase. He pulled me back to our dressing room and slid inside me, soft and sweet, as my husband.

He made meaningful love to his wife for the first time and it was sweet enough that I felt the tears stream down my cheeks after I came and his lips kissed them away as he came.

Then Shay had to be called in to, yet again, fix my makeup... and my hair.

"Girl, I'd be bitching if I didn't just get some myself," she said, wiggling her eyebrows. "Thank goodness these halls are full of coat and cleaning closets. And after that fucking wedding, girl," she said, wiping at my smudged mascara, "trust me, Jake and I weren't the only ones getting our romance on."

Freshened up, Chase led me down to the reception where we danced to a song he picked and it was the first song from the first playlist I ever put on.

Coffeehouse music. But it was a soft and sweet, crooning singer-songwriter love song and it just... fit.

We were making our rounds at the tables, Chase with a possessive arm around my hips, half hauling my body against his as he did most of the talking, when the minister caught us.

"You know, I never got a chance to ask," he started, face animated and open, "how did you two meet?" I turned slightly, looking up at Chase as he looked down at me, light in both of our eyes before we threw our heads back and laughed.

It was right in that moment that the photographer snapped a picture of us.

It was the picture we had framed and hung over our fireplace. It was the picture I stared at every morning, sometimes with Chase wrapped around me from behind, sometimes with our daughter on my hip, sometimes with our grandbabies at my feet. Always, always with love swelling my heart so full it was a wonder it didn't explode.

xx

Don't Forget

<u>Dear Reader,</u>
Thank you for taking time out of your life to read this book. If you loved this book, I would really appreciate it if you could hop onto Goodreads or Amazon and tell me your favorite parts. You can also spread the word by recommending the book to friends or sending digital copies that can be received via kindle or kindle app on any device.

Also by Jessica Gadziala

**If you liked this book, check out these other series
and titles in the NAVESINK BANK UNIVERSE:**

The Henchmen MC
Reign
Cash
Wolf
Repo
Duke
Renny
Lazarus
Pagan
Cyrus
Edison
Reeve
Sugar
The Fall of V
Adler
Roderick
Virgin
Roan
Camden

The Savages
Monster
Killer
Savior

Mallick Brothers
For A Good Time, Call
Shane
Ryan
Mark
Eli
Charlie & Helen: Back to the Beginning

Investigators
367 Days
14 Weeks
4 Months

Dark
Dark Mysteries
Dark Secrets
Dark Horse

Professionals
The Fixer
The Ghost
The Messenger
The General
The Babysitter
The Middle Man

Rivers Brothers
Lift You Up

STANDALONES WITHIN NAVESINK BANK:
Vigilante
Grudge Match

OTHER SERIES AND STANDALONES:

Stars Landing
What The Heart Needs
What The Heart Wants
What The Heart Finds
What The Heart Knows
The Stars Landing Deviant
What The Heart Learns

Surrogate
The Sex Surrogate
Dr. Chase Hudson

The Green Series
Into the Green
Escape from the Green

DEBT
Dissent
Stuffed: A Thanksgiving Romance
Unwrapped
Peace, Love, & Macarons
A Navesink Bank Christmas
Don't Come
Fix It Up
N.Y.E.
faire l'amour

Revenge

About the Author

Jessica Gadziala is a full-time writer, parrot enthusiast, and coffee drinker from New Jersey. She enjoys short rides to the book store, sad songs, and cold weather.

She is very active on Goodreads, Facebook, as well as her personal groups on those sites. Join in. She's friendly.

Stalk Her!

Connect with Jessica:

Facebook: https://www.facebook.com/JessicaGadziala/
Facebook Group:
https://www.facebook.com/groups/314540025563403/

Goodreads:
https://www.goodreads.com/author/show/13800950.Jessica_Gadziala
Goodreads Group:
https://www.goodreads.com/group/show/177944-jessica-gadziala-books-and-bullsh

Twitter: @JessicaGadziala

JessicaGadziala.com

<3/ Jessica

CPSIA information can be obtained
at www.ICGtesting.com
Printed in the USA
BVHW041030110423
662130BV00006B/98